Trouble You Don't Knead

A Laughing Loaf Bakery Mystery

Book 3

Victoria Kazarian

To the creatives:
Human heart speaks to human heart.
You will never be replaced.

Chapter One

It was 6:59 a.m. on a chilly October morning in River Grove.

The high schoolers started lining up at the bakery at 6:45 a.m., backpacks and messenger bags over their shoulders as they waited outside. Their breath froze and drifted up in cloudy puffs as they talked and gestured excitedly.

As soon as I opened the front door of the bakery, that characteristic River Grove fall smell drifted in: wood smoke, damp leaves, and the smell of newly washed flannel shirts. Before I got the door fully open, a dozen or so teenagers raced past me to nab tables in the dining area.

"Hey! No running," I barked as I watched them pass. "There's room for everyone. Slow down."

I set the joke of the day on its stand on the counter.

Laughing Loaf Joke of the Day
Why did the Invisible Man turn down the job offer?
He couldn't see himself doing it.

Then I took my place behind the counter as my

assistant manager, Beck Rodriguez, manned the espresso machine. Beck made espresso drinks fast and her ability to multitask with orders amazed me.

"A Cherry Orchard Latte and an order of French Toast Sticks," our first customer, a young woman in a UC Santa Cruz hoodie, said breathlessly as she pulled cash out of her duct tape wallet. The teenaged boy next to her gave her a coy smile. She punched him in the arm and laughed. "Okay, *two* Cherry Orchard Lattes. You so owe me, Zack."

"Coming right up." Beck nodded and started in on the drinks. I began filling clamshell containers with the French toast sticks and inserting cups of vanilla spice syrup in each, before separating cinnamon rolls for quick packaging. These were by far the most popular orders for the high school crowd.

The French toast sticks were another of Beck's inventions. She'd been thinking of the high schoolers and how they might need a finger-food breakfast they could eat while studying or on their way to school. Along with the accompanying vanilla spice syrup, they'd become a big hit, especially between the hours of 7 and 8 a.m.

As of September 1, we'd expanded our hours at The Laughing Loaf Bakery. We now opened the doors at 7 a.m. to a crowd of teenagers—an hour earlier than our previous start time. This sometimes drove Beck and I to the point of near exhaustion by 10:30 a.m., but we were doing great business.

The Laughing Loaf was located three blocks from River Grove High School, and we'd always gotten students dashing in that last half-hour before school for breakfast and coffee. I decided an earlier opening was going to bring in more business, and Beck and I made changes to accommodate it–coming in earlier and doing more setup and planning the day before.

Since they had to be at school by 8:30, the students were usually gone before the older River Grovians came in for their coffee. Though the teenagers did socialize loudly—I don't think I've heard anything louder than a group of teenaged girls laughing at some juicy gossip—most of them were there to finish their homework. Once they got their drinks and food, the noise level usually dropped considerably.

This morning, the big, round table in the center of the dining area filled up quickly. Backpacks were plunked on the table, notebooks taken out, phones quickly checked for the latest texts from friends. Chloe Westerman, the police chief's granddaughter, was whispering excitedly to a friend across the table, pausing occasionally to dip a French toast stick in syrup and gobble it down.

By 8:15, the students had finished their breakfasts and were loading up their backpacks, as the line of adults started to form.

I took a sip of my spice latte, our featured drink for fall, and after the morning crowd had thinned at Laughing Loaf Bakery, I sat down for a mini-break. I stifled a yawn and took one last gulp. My little dog, Biga, and I had been at the bakery since 4:30 a.m. Today would be a marathon for me. After closing up, I'd drive my maybe-boyfriend, Nate Behrens, to San Francisco International Airport. He was flying to the Galapagos Islands for a photo shoot for a British naturalist's coffee table book. I felt pretty down about him leaving, even for a week. The past few months we'd seen each other almost every day.

Today's cooler air and overcast skies made me want to cozy things up with baked goods. I wanted to bake them, and happily, customers wanted to eat them. I welcomed the cooler weather after one of the hottest summers on record in River Grove.

Hands down, fall has always been my favorite time of year, with the start of a new school year and my own memories of buying school supplies and starting new classes. It's a season for new things. My heart beats faster in the fall.

Today, people lingered at the outside tables in down jackets, talking with friends while their dogs lapped at the water bowls I'd started setting out in the mornings. It was a sweet sight, a glimpse of community. You wouldn't know that this small town had been the site of two murders just three months ago. Or that I'd received a terrifying letter written in Russian. A letter that made me wonder how long my father, my dog, and I would be able to stay in this quaint town.

At 9:30, Annie and Eric Morgan came in for coffee with their dog, Pixie, an Irish wolfhound who was anything but pixie sized. He was the size of a small pony. While Beck worked on frying up the day's last batch of beignets in the back room, I got up to serve the couple. The Morgans were some of the bakery's biggest supporters. Normally, one of them watched Pixie outside, while the other came in and ordered. Today, Pixie trotted in with them expectantly. Then she sat down next to Annie as if she were planning to stay for a while.

"I'm sorry, Gracie." Annie said apologetically. "Normally, we wouldn't bring her in, but she had a vet visit yesterday and is feeling a little needy today. I hope it's okay."

I glanced back anxiously in the direction of the back room, where Biga was walking the limits of his gated area, like a prisoner in outside time. His last interaction with

Pixie hadn't been great, though it wasn't Pixie's fault. When it came to big dogs, Biga had a major chip on his shoulder.

"That should be fine," I said with a smile as I worked on their lattes at the espresso machine. Hopefully, Biga would be back in his cage watching Beck and would be unaware of the dog's presence.

Suddenly, Pixie began a low, deep growl. She got up on all fours, ready to investigate.

Soon Biga in the back room began growling then let out one of his odd Basenji-style yelps. Then both dogs launched into full-on barking, outraged at each other's presence, though they couldn't even see each other. How do dogs do this?

Kimmy Anderson and her daughter, Lucy, who were drinking apple juice and reading books in the dining area, looked up, startled and a little frightened.

"Sorry about that, Gracie." Eric Morgan quickly took Pixie out. As Eric pulled him out the door, the dog strained on his leash and Eric struggled to keep him under control.

"Pixie didn't do anything wrong." I sighed as I set their two lattes down on the counter. "Biga gets territorial about the bakery. He weighs twelve pounds but he's got a thing for dogs bigger than he is. He thinks he can take them on."

"Pixie's usually pretty easygoing." Annie looked out the bakery window with concern at the large, hairy grey dog. She lowered her voice as she leaned over the counter. "I think he's just off because of the *V-E-T*. Thanks for understanding, Gracie." She took the coffees with her, leaning her back against the front door to open it as she headed for Eric and the table he'd claimed outside.

With no other customers in sight, I headed for the back room to give my little dog a lecture. And a treat—because when it comes to Biga, I'm a big softie.

Beck was tending a cluster of beignets bobbing in a hot pot of oil on the stove. The air smelled like deep-fried, sugary goodness, like a donut shop—only better. As I passed his gated area, Biga looked up at me, flashing big innocent eyes, as if he hadn't just been barking furiously a few minutes ago.

I squatted down next to his pen. "Silly boy. What would you do if someone *did* attack us? Bark them to death? You've got an annoying bark, so maybe you could do it." I picked him up and carried him around the room for a bit. He nudged his head under my arm, trying to burrow into me.

"Fine. Want a treat?"

Biga's ears perked up like radar dishes angling toward a signal. I laid him down in the pen and went to get him one of his chicken treats from my closet-sized office.

As she fished the beignets out of the oil with a slotted spoon, Beck laughed. "Like you even have to ask him?"

I held the treat over his head.

"Now—up." I called out, and the pup stood up on back legs like a circus dog. I broke the treat in half, and he grabbed the bite from my hand. "Now, sit." Obediently, Biga sat down and looked up at me sweetly with a slight tilt to his head, as if he'd never misbehaved in his life. I let him have the other half.

The front doorbell tinkled, and I patted my little Chihuahua-Basenji mix pup and went to wash my hands. By the sound of the voices, I could tell who it was: River Grove's crime-fighting duo, Police Chief Westerman and Mayor Corinne Webster, aka Mayor C.

"I expected you two in here earlier this morning," I said good-naturedly to the pair, who usually came in right after 8 a.m. and took the corner table.

The chief leaned forward, ogling the display case. "Our power went out this morning. I had to get the generator going, and I never did get my breakfast. Have any beignets left?"

Power outages were a common occurrence in the Santa Cruz mountains, and with River Grove's off-the-beaten-path location, it could be hours—sometimes days—until crews came out to get things going again.

"Beck's finishing up a batch in the back room." I nodded and started up the espresso machine. "They'll be fresh and very hot."

Mayor C grimaced at the chief. "Dave, a diet of those isn't going to keep you fit," she said sternly. She turned to me, a look of superiority on her face. "Oat milk latte and a kale tarragon cup for me, please."

In the back room, Beck had the fresh beignets laid out on a baking rack and had just brushed them with a light coating of honey.

"Let me get these ready for you." She reached for the shaker of powdered sugar, dusting three with a light coating of snowy sweetness.

I placed the three beignets on a plate and brought them up front.

"Now there we go," the chief's eyes followed the plate of fried treats until I set it down on the counter, next to their drinks. "That's what I'm talking about."

"What are you two up to today? Any news in town I should be aware of?" I asked the two town officials.

I was half-kidding. The two of them had each come to me separately to ask for advice during a murder case this summer, when they weren't speaking to each other. But they'd resumed their crimefighting partnership and were back to gathering here every weekday to discuss public safety issues over breakfast. If anything was going on in town now, they'd keep it to themselves.

"As a matter of fact, the mayor and I are working on traffic issues," the chief said, lifting a beignet to his mouth.

"There's a traffic problem?" I asked, handing the mayor and the chief their lattes.

"Whenever Highway 17 is backed up, people think they can cut through River Grove on their way to the coast," Mayor C said. "It's causing a disruption downtown. Not to mention bringing in undesirables. We're going to put an end to it."

Many people on their way to the Santa Cruz Boardwalk and the beaches did turn off on Highway 9 to avoid traffic on the more crowded Highway 17, especially in the summer. As a result, there were days when it took fifteen minutes instead of five to get through downtown. But sometimes those people did stop and spend money in our little town.

The mayor and the chief took their lattes over to the corner table and soon they were in animated conversation. After their falling out this summer, it made me feel good to see them together and busying themselves with something as mundane as traffic control. The rash of murders earlier this year was unsettling, but it could be a "statistical anomaly," as my professor father had called it.

Things did seem to be improving in River Grove. Bakery customers lingered over conversations in the dining area, possibly drawn closer to each other after the year's scary events. After a year and a half in business, the bakery was finally making a modest profit. Recently I'd even met a few out-of-towners visiting the bakery.

As I sipped my spice latte, I made a mental list of what I'd need to get done this afternoon. Beck was working longer hours and was here for more of the afternoon prep, taking a big load off me. Today, she'd close up, since I had to leave by 2 p.m. to drive Nate Behrens to the airport.

Between Nate going away, and the disturbing letter I'd received a few months ago, I was feeling down. Apparently, I was doing a bad job of hiding it.

Beck brought out the beignets and a tray of cinnamon rolls and began refilling the display case. She glanced over the counter at me, a look of concern on her face.

"You okay, Gracie? You've been quiet today."

I'd tried to stay upbeat at the bakery, but I had a lot on my mind. Some of what was on my mind, I couldn't talk about to Beck or anyone in River Grove except my father.

"It's Nate, isn't it?" Beck studied my face looking for clues.

Realistically, I would miss Nate.

"Sure." I kept a smile on my face as I nodded at her. "That's probably it."

Nate and I had grown closer over the past few months. We'd come a long way since we first met. Grieving after his brother Nico's murder, he'd seemed like a hostile, unpleasant person to me. It had taken me a while to see how much the murder had affected him. I found out there was more to him than I'd thought.

Entering a new relationship scared the heck out of me. I'd left Seattle two years ago after I found out my husband was not who I thought he was. With that behind me, all I wanted to do was bake, hang out with my dog, and enjoy the comforts of my small new community.

"Nate'll be back in like a week, right?" Beck said cheerfully as she prepared to head to the back room. "I'm sure he'll have lots of stories to tell about his time there. Absence makes the heart grow fonder, that's what my mother always says."

I'd never understood that saying. It didn't seem like it applied to me right now. Of course, the absence *could* make me realize I really did not want a relationship.

Whether I wanted to admit it or not, I'd become close to the guy. I'd miss walking with him and Biga in the evenings and getting excited text alerts that he'd spotted some new bird in the forest. *Stop everything! I've just found a California Thrasher. Listen to this. Isn't his song amazing?*

There was something endearing about this stocky, muscular guy coming to life when he set eyes on a tiny fragile little bird.

Since I was in witness protection, there was a lot I couldn't share with Nate. I wondered if I had any right to be in a relationship with him. I couldn't tell him who I really was.

Two years ago, my life had changed completely.

I'd found out that my husband Ben, a software engineer who worked for a defense contractor, had been selling secrets to foreign governments with his college friend, Kyle Burnett. I'd found the files in a folder on Ben's computer labeled FANTASY FOOTBALL LEAGUE. There was a spreadsheet with names, transactions and large amounts of money that had been moved into Ben's personal account. Foreign names I didn't recognize. While Ben played a video game with Kyle and his little brother in the other room, I went over the names, amounts, and dates. The large amounts coincided with times Ben had made or talked about making large purchases: our sailboat, a planned trip to Africa, and house hunting on Mercer Island—an expensive suburb of Seattle on an island in the middle of Lake Washington.

I copied everything from Ben's folder onto a thumb drive, while the guys laughed and hooted over the video game in the other room.

After a difficult conversation with Ben and a night of soul searching, I got up the next morning, put my little dog in his crate, packed some clothes in my gym bag, and left the house.

I met with the FBI and told them what I'd found.

The FBI followed the trail of money and within a day, Ben and his friend were arrested. I testified about what I'd found in federal court. I got horrible looks from Ben and from Kyle's family, who assumed I made the spy story up. After the trials that convicted Ben and then Kyle, my father and I were accepted into the federal witness protection program, WITSEC.

The marshals moved us into a house in an undisclosed location for the trials. I remember my last day in the house Ben and I had bought together. Ben was in jail, awaiting trial. The house felt eerie, haunted. I quickly gathered up my recipe notebooks and sourdough starter, Biga's toys, and anything I wanted to salvage from my life in Seattle.

Federal marshals gave me, my professor father, and even my dog, new names and identities. We needed them; there were foreign governments who were not happy I'd shut down their flow of information.

We were relocated from Seattle to River Grove, a small town in Northern California's Santa Cruz mountains. I felt safe in this small town in the redwoods, and I'd even made friends, like Elana Schiffer, who'd bonded with me over our mutual love of wine and food. I wasn't able to tell my new friend much about myself and my past, except the backstory the marshals had given me.

Now a letter with a Russian stamp I'd received in the

mail three months ago made me wonder if we were no longer safe in River Grove.

The federal marshals in charge of our case were concerned.

One evening six weeks ago, the two marshals assigned to us drove up to our place in River Grove to interview us, and discuss the results of their investigation into the letter. As not to arouse suspicion, they pulled up in front of our house in a beat-up white Ford pickup truck, country music blaring, with logos from tourist sites pasted to the bumper. They'd ditched their navy suits and black Lincoln Continental in order to blend in with the residents of the mountain town of River Grove.

Their new look did *not* fit the two very formal agents, and I suppressed a giggle when I saw them.

Federal Agent Jeremy LaValle wore faded jeans and a t-shirt with a beer logo instead of his stiff, black, tailored suit; the only thing that revealed he wasn't a local yokel was the rock-hard abs visible under his shirt. Surly Agent Maura Piccelli's black hair was pulled up in a bouncy pony tail. She wore a ruffly yellow sundress that looked like she'd sewed it herself from a Simplicity pattern.

Agent Piccelli stood in our entry way, eyes darting around the living room. She walked over to the hall leading to the bedrooms, basically casing the place. "We need a room with no windows—or one with shades over the windows." Even in our isolated house in River Grove, the marshals thought it was important to avoid prying eyes.

I nodded. "Let's use my father's office." I led them back to the small room packed with my father's desk and computer and lined with bookshelves. I brought in some of our kitchen chairs. I felt the desire to hand Agent LaValle a bottle of Miller Light, to go with his new look. We settled into the cramped space, our knees almost touching.

"Jonathan, Gracie," Agent LaValle looked at us, his chiseled jaw clenched. He seemed ready to deliver a stern lecture. Biga sat on my father's lap, casting suspicious looks at these two strangers. "I need to ask if either of you could possibly have told anyone your old names."

Both agents looked at us sternly, with a look of firm authority that clashed with their casual attire.

"Could you have let slip *anything* about your past to anyone in town?" He asked. "We need to know this in order to protect you."

I knew I hadn't, but I worried about my father, who could be absent-minded sometimes, as he spent most of his days immersed in his theoretical physics readings. I worried that maybe after a glass of wine he'd mentioned something about his past to the woman in town he'd been dating on and off, Mary Jo Hartman.

"I haven't," I said, thinking of all the times I'd wanted to tell Elana or Nate about my past. "I've been especially careful."

My father let out a laugh, but it was a nervous one. "My daughter makes sure I keep my mouth shut. At the dinner table, she grills me every few days on our backstory. I'm British. You must know I don't give out personal information."

Agent LaValle gave us a dry look. "We want to make sure you are both taking this seriously. WITSEC has never lost a witness. We want to keep it that way. This is a voluntary program, and you are free to leave it at any time. You both know the risks. Gracie, your testimony brought down a spy network. We know this hasn't been easy for you. We thank you for your help and sacrifice."

My heart pounded. Turning in Ben and his coworker Kyle was great for the country, but I was afraid we'd be paying for this for the rest of our (hopefully long) lives. Although, going into WITSEC might have been easier for my father and I since we didn't have an extended family to break ties with.

I had friends in Seattle, but most of my time had been spent at my tech job and with my husband Ben. The longer I lived in River Grove, the more I realized that leaving both behind had changed my life for the better.

"What can you tell us about the letter?" I asked, trying to keep my teeth from chattering with nervousness. "Who sent it? What did it say exactly?"

Agent LaValle's lips tightened. "It's a threat. I can't tell you any more than that. We're handling it and feel confident about our ability to keep you safe. We have an operative nearby, who's keeping an eye out for you and is on call 24/7. We're monitoring communications across our networks and checking in with our local sources. We've been looking for anything related to you, your father, and your location. So far, we have found almost nothing. We'll keep tuning in."

Almost nothing? I shifted in my seat. This was not reassuring.

Agent Piccelli exchanged a significant look with LaValle. I felt my stomach sink.

"Considering what a blow your husband's arrest was to the intelligence efforts of several countries, the communication channels have been very quiet." Agent Piccelli solemnly tucked a renegade curl back into her perky pony tail. "This could mean these agencies have cut their losses and moved on. It could also mean the letter came from someone who doesn't use standard communication channels."

Her lips turned down as she nodded. The foreboding look on her face clashed with her cheery yellow sundress. She looked to me, then to my father.

"I'm talking about someone at the top."

Over the next few months, I thought about what the marshals had said. As my bakery continued to grow in popularity in River Grove and beyond, I wondered.

How long would my place of safety last?

Chapter Two

After taking Biga home to spend the rest of the day with my father, I went to the back room and prepared to bake brioche loaves.

I'd mixed a bigger batch of dough this time, since Beck had been using day-old brioche loaves for the French toast sticks. The sweet, buttery smell of the brioche loaves baking was one of the best advertisements we had for the bakery, as it drifted out into the downtown like a subliminal bread beacon. People would pop in and start looking at the bread case, convinced that they needed a loaf of bread for dinner or the next morning's breakfast.

"You still need two of the brioche loaves?" I asked Beck, who'd just finished chopping kale and tarragon for tomorrow's kale tarragon frittata cups—our new healthy breakfast choice. She dumped the earthy, fragrant greenery into plastic bags and took them to the fridge.

"I may not use all of them tomorrow," Beck said, returning to the metal worktable. "But I can always cut the sticks and freeze them for another day."

The cold weather, and perhaps my anxieties about the

letter, made me want to go full introvert and plunge into my first baking love: bread. I'd grown up baking bread with my father in high school. It had been a comforting hobby for both of us after my mother passed away.

Now I wanted to sink my hands into rich, brown dough, hearty and nutty. This week I'd introduce a loaf I used to make in the fall in Seattle: whole wheat biga with raisins, molasses, and walnuts. It had been my fall go-to lunch on cold, rainy days. I took it with me to my old job as a tech project manager: lunch was a thick slice of buttered whole wheat biga bread and a thermos of sweet-savory butternut squash soup.

After lunch, I'd mix the biga-- the pre-ferment-- for my first batch of the bread.

"Gracie, I can't believe I forgot to tell you!" Beck looked up excitedly as she piled loaves onto the cart to refill the showcase. "Sam said someone in his work crew in San Jose knew about The Laughing Loaf."

I slid two trays of brioche loaves into the oven.

"Oh yeah?" I hummed as I shut the oven door. "Had he been by the bakery?"

"He read about it in the *Mercury News*. One of their food writers stopped here when passing through town. She was very sneaky. I didn't even realize she was from a newspaper. In the article, she recommended the bakery as a good place to stop on the way to the beach." Beck's black eyes snapped with excitement. "Isn't that amazing? It's not just people in River Grove that know about us now."

Good news. As long as it was The Laughing Loaf and not its owner that everyone knew about.

"I've talked to a few customers from out of town in the past couple of weeks," I said as I shaped the smooth, warm dough into loaves. "Mystery solved. That's where they heard about us."

"You must be so happy, Gracie." Beck said as she began wiping down the metal table. "You started Laughing Loaf only a year and a half ago and look how well we're doing."

There was a residue of anxiety in my mind right now, but, as always, Beck's enthusiasm couldn't help but lift my spirits.

"Okay, I guess that's something to be happy about. But you're a part of that, too." I set the industrial oven to preheat. "I don't think we'd be doing this well if it wasn't for you."

Beck laughed and turned pink. "Thank you. I love working here."

I checked the big industrial clock on the wall over the old aqua fridge. 1:30. Time to pack up. I'd leave Beck to take out the brioche loaves and close and set the bakery up for tomorrow.

I had a man to take to the airport.

Nate Behrens was waiting outside the bakery on his bike, a canvas backpack on his back—all the luggage he'd need for his trip. I had a feeling he and I packed for trips very differently.

I watched the muscles move in his massive shoulders as he took off the pack and felt that fluttery feeling inside again.

He grinned at me and gave me a hug that lasted long enough for my legs to feel rubbery.

"I probably look a little crazy. I wasn't able to get out on the bike today, so I thought I'd ride down here. Okay if I store my bike here till I get back? If not, no problem. I'll ask Sam Rodriguez to come pick it up."

I laughed. "You *would* ride your bike here while

wearing all your luggage for a week's trip." I opened the front door of the bakery and waved him in. "Bring it in. I've got a spot for it in the storeroom." He wheeled the bike in and propped it up on the wall opposite my flour bins.

Beck cheerfully made us lattes for the road. She tried to craft a bird in latte foam on Nate's, and it turned out actually looking like one. We took off, driving up Highway 1 until we crossed over to Interstate 280 via the twisting Highway 92, which passed by farmlands and lush green hillsides on its way from the coast to the San Francisco Bay. Nate was brimming with excitement about this trip, his first to the Galapagos Islands. He talked about the finches he'd be photographing and how they prompted the first theories of the survival of the fittest. Finches with different shapes of beaks were able to access certain types of food in hard times and survive. Those birds reproduced others with the same genetic makeup. Nate described trying to capture birds in movement. And how that perfect shot wasn't a matter of luck; he usually took hundreds of photos to find it.

We were halfway to the airport when he turned to me with a sheepish look. "I just realized I've been talking the whole time." He rubbed the back of his neck. "I'd like to know how you are, Gracie. You've been so quiet lately."

Was I that obvious? Beck and Nate had both noticed it. I'd thought I was pretty good at keeping my secrets hidden.

"A lot going on at the bakery, I guess. I'm coming in at 4:30, since we're opening earlier. It's a really long day." And I remembered how I'd been able to share my *feelings* truthfully to my best friend, Elana, earlier this year without telling her anything I was supposed to keep secret. "Also it's been an intense year. It's all hitting me now, if that makes sense." It was true. Everything I'd been through in the past two years *was* piling up on me now. The shock of who my ex-husband Ben really was, the hours of court testimony, the plunge into a new life and identity. It felt like too much.

We rode together quietly for the rest of the trip. It was a comfortable silence, and I didn't feel the need to say anything to make conversation. When we pulled up to International Departures at SFO, I wheeled the Subaru in as close as I could to the curb, wedging it in nicely between two cars being unloaded.

"Well done, Gracie." Nate looked at me with admiration and gave me an air high five.

While an airport security guard headed toward the car, ready to tell me to move on, Nate leaned across the gear shift, and as I as moved in, gave me a long, deep kiss. In the corner of my eye, I saw the guard wait awkwardly, trying to look elsewhere. When Nate pulled away from me, he tapped insistently on the window.

Nate opened the door and gave the guard a big grin that said, *sorry, not sorry.*

Then he pulled his pack out of the back seat of the car, smiled at me and headed inside the terminal, merging with the crowd of travelers.

With the memory of that kiss, the first one Nate had given me that wasn't a peck, I drove back home in a haze as thick as the coastal fog.

Nice parting gift, Mr. Behrens.

The roads were dark now, which I didn't mind. The lights of houses sparkled in the blackness like jewels sprinkled over the hills. Highway 92 curved in front of me, lit by my headlights, and it looked dreamy. Highway 1 along the coast was dark, and I swore I heard the faint sound of the waves hitting the beaches, though I couldn't see them in the darkness. I remembered walking on the beach once in the dark; the foam tipping the waves was almost luminescent in the darkness, glowing like Cheshire Cat's teeth.

I turned onto Highway 9, and entered the redwoods, with few cars on the curving highway. I'd be home for a late dinner with my father, who'd volunteered to cook for us tonight. He'd been coming along nicely after the lessons I gave him. Tonight he announced dinner would be pasta with prepared marinara sauce I'd frozen a few weeks ago, so he should do fine. I loved that I wasn't the one cooking dinner every night. It took such a weight off my shoulders. I'd felt responsible for him after my mother's death. Before I married Ben, I'd done all the cooking for him. Since we moved to River Grove, I'd gotten back in the habit of preparing meals for us. I realized that after closing up at the bakery, I had very little time to myself. That had to change.

I drove through downtown—all dark, with only Riverside Saloon and RG's Pizza lit up. Everything else closed down at 6 p.m. River Grove was one of those towns that rolled up its streets around sundown every night. Aside from the pizza parlor and the saloon, there wasn't much of a night life in town.

I drove past the edge of town to Pilgrim Way, our street, and followed it to the end. On this cold night, everyone was huddled inside. There were lights in windows, people moving around inside, happy and warm. Wood smoke drifted up from chimneys, filling the air with the scents of fall. I'd get a fire going in the woodstove myself once I got inside.

As I pulled into the carport, I saw something strange moving at the edge of our property, a few trees away from the river. It could be a person, but I told myself it could just as easily be a racoon or mountain lion. That made more sense. They'd been coming further and further into town every year.

My body seemed to think otherwise; a prickly feeling on my arms and neck told me it was human.

I parked, turned off my car lights and grabbed a flashlight from my glove compartment. I sat in the darkness of the car as I watched for more movement. Soon I saw that the shape was a person, and it was moving toward our front porch. I beat on the car horn as hard as I could and leaped out of my car with the flashlight.

"Hey!" I yelled into the darkness.

I heard a rustle in the underbrush, footsteps running. I shined my flashlight in the direction of the noise and the light caught a person in a long coat hunched over, making their way to the trail.

I began following—walking along the line of trees that paralleled the river.

I shined the flashlight over the path ahead, but now the only movement I saw was branches waving in the wind. The trail was empty.

In the distance, I heard an engine start.

Tires squealed, as whoever had been skulking around outside our house sped away into the night.

Chapter Three

My father stirred a pan of pasta in the kitchen while listening to a lecture from last year's Nobel Prize winner in Physics. He hadn't even heard the noise of me beating on the horn. That's the nice thing about being as oblivious as my father—you don't experience the same level of anxiety as someone like me.

Biga, too, was unbothered. He'd curled up in his bed on the floor of the dining room, occasionally raising his head to see if scraps or crumbs had dropped on the floor.

"Hello, dear." My father turned to me with a smile, a smudge of tomato sauce on his cheek. "Did you see Nate off?"

I nodded. At this point, my hands and jaw were shaking, which he did notice. He frowned. "Are you quite all right, dear?"

"When I pulled into the carport, I saw someone heading for our porch. I chased them down to the r-river." My teeth were chattering. I reached into my purse and pulled out my phone. "I need to call the chief."

Ten minutes later, Deputy Brad Castro pulled up to the

house in his pickup truck, wearing jeans and a Metallica t-shirt, smelling like he'd just showered and applied enough aftershave to knock out a horse.

"Chief said you had a prowler," he said gruffly at the door, not looking particularly happy to be there. "He's at his grandson's school open house, so he sent me. I just got off my shift at Best Buy and was out to dinner with Briana."

I invited him in.

"Brad, you want any pasta and garlic bread?" My dad gestured to the table, where he'd just set a basket of buttery, very garlicky bread. Brad looked longingly at the basket. I heard his stomach rumble.

"No, thank you, Mr. Markley. I gotta take care of this and get back to RG's Pizza. My girlfriend Briana and I were waiting for our order." Brad turned to me. "Tell me what you saw, Gracie."

My shaking had subsided, and it was easier to get words out. I told the deputy what I'd seen and how I'd tried to follow whoever it was, then heard a car start and squeal away.

"You know what the chief would tell you, Gracie." He gave me a disapproving look. "It's a real bad idea to follow it up on your own. You know how mad he gets when you do this. I'll go out and see what I can find," he said, as he pulled out his phone and texted someone, presumably Briana. "Let me get my belt from the truck."

Brad left and began searching our property, with a flashlight and a gun on his belt. I knew the prowler was gone, but it made me feel better that he was out there--even though no serious thief or prowler was going to be scared off by a 21-year-old kid who worked part-time as a security guard at Best Buy.

My dad and I sat down at the table and started eating.

My dad had done a good job with the meal. He'd made the garlic bread from a Laughing Loaf sourdough loaf, and the butter and garlic had sunk into every pore of the slices. My breath was going to reek, but I wouldn't be kissing anyone for a week, anyway. I didn't care. The pasta was delicious and cooked *al dente*. He'd made us each a "salad." It was just a few baby carrots and celery chunks in a bowl, but he'd gotten some vegetables into the meal. And they weren't his preferred ones, peas and potatoes.

The meal was good. I didn't have much of an appetite tonight.

My father watched me pick at the pasta. He finished his and sat back in his chair, a serious look on his face.

"You think this has something to do with the letter?"

I put my napkin next to my plate. "I don't know. But we do know someone in Russia knows who we are and where we live."

"It's been three months since you got the letter," my father said. "Nothing's happened, Gracie. The agents said they haven't picked up anything in their communication channels."

Unlike me, my father tended to be oblivious and optimistic. *Oh, so nothing's happened yet? I'll get back to my reading then.*

I couldn't live this way.

I wished I could talk about this with Elana Schiffer, my best friend in River Grove. I couldn't.

I wished I could tell Nate about this. He wasn't here, and even if he was, I couldn't tell him about the letter or reveal our secret identities.

As we finished the last bites of our "salad," Brad knocked on the door—calling out his name loudly to make sure we knew it was him. He was wearing nitrile gloves and holding something in a plastic bag.

"The footprints in the mud look fresh. Looks like he wore boots. And I found this near the river, a few yards from your house." He held up the bag. I looked closely and saw some crumpled white plastic candy wrappers. They had foreign writing on it. I was expecting it to be Russian, but it looked like Chinese characters. I couldn't think of anyone in River Grove who would have something like this. To be fair, out-of-towners did sometimes visit River Grove and the San Luciano River, coming from San Jose or the peninsula. The south bay had a vibrant population of first- and second-generation Chinese immigrants. Anyone could have brought along treats they'd bought at the Asian markets in the area.

"Thanks, Brad." I felt relieved. Maybe the wrappers had been there for months. Maybe they had nothing to do with the information my ex-husband Ben and his friend Kyle had sold to not only Russia, but China and other countries.

"If you see someone poking around your house, call us. Don't go chasing them yourself. One of us will come out." Brad frowned as he lectured me sternly. "And keep your doors and windows locked. Some people in River Grove still leave everything open and unlocked like in the old days." He shook his head, then I heard his phone buzz. He checked his texts. "That's Briana. Pizza's ready."

When he'd left, I started clearing the table—I was on cleanup since my father had done the cooking.

"I feel a little better." I said as my father grabbed a sheaf of papers and went to his big recliner to read. "It's still disturbing that someone was lurking around our property."

"Could it have been some kid, out exploring." My father

said, his voice trailing off. I was quickly losing him to the book he'd started leafing through.

As I began rinsing dishes, I thought about the roots we'd put down in this town. The bakery I ran, that had become a place for the people of River Grove to hang out. My new career as a baker was much more satisfying than tracking tech projects on spreadsheets, which I'd done in my project management job in Seattle. I loved feeding the people. I thought of my assistant bakery manager Beck and how much fun it was to work with her and see her grow in her skills.

And then there was my friend Elana. We'd grown close over the past year and a half. Even though I couldn't tell her everything going on in my life, or anything about my past, we were becoming close friends.

I'd been so busy (and exhausted) for the past month, I hadn't been able to find a date for Elana and I to go do something fun. It was something I needed. Judging by how frustrating her job had been lately, she needed it, too.

I texted her.

> I need some fun! Grab drinks at Riverside? Friday?

> Please! Work's been awful.

> Then we REALLY need to do this. Meet you at 7.

> Missing Nate?

> Not at all

> LIAR

Chapter Four

The next morning, I got up at 3:45 a.m., anxious to get my whole wheat biga loaves prepared for baking, as well as everything else we needed for our 7 a.m opening.

My little dog wedged in next to me like a warm little lump all night. He wasn't as excited as I was about getting up. He surveyed me with a bored look, then burrowed back into the blankets.

As usual, as soon as I got dressed and tied on my work apron, Biga's head popped up. I recognized his look of FOMO. He leaped off the bed and let me put him into his crate for the ride to the bakery. He wasn't going to miss out on treats or on the loving attention Beck would give him.

It felt dim and bleak outside, as cloud cover blocked out the light of the stars. On clear nights when it wasn't foggy, stars burned brightly in the sky, out here away from the light pollution of a city. The air felt cold and slightly damp this morning. I shivered as I unlocked the back door of the bakery, Biga's crate in hand. I immediately switched on all the lights and locked the back door. I had an urge to turn on the heat, but I knew as soon as I got the oven started, the back room would warm up just fine.

I reached up to the storage rack above the proofer to turn on the music, an upbeat playlist of dance music I'd set up yesterday. Immediately the thump of the music got me going.

After last night's scare, I needed my comforting morning routine.

I set out a water bowl and a bowl of kibbles in his pen, then set Biga down in it and tossed in a rubber dog toy, which bounced with a squeak, then rolled away from him. He immediately attacked it and began wrestling it into submission like a growling goblin.

"Biga, thanks for taking care of that horrible threat to our safety. What would I do without you?"

After scrubbing my hands, I floured the surface of the metal table and began pulling bannetons, the baskets that hold loaves as they rise, out of the proofer. I turned each one out onto the table then shaped each of the whole wheat dough balls into tight, round boules. I placed them on the sheet for one last rise before baking. I'd make a dozen on this first run, then see the reception they got from my customers. I couldn't wait to smell them baking. With the raisins, molasses, walnuts, and nutty whole wheat flavor, they were the perfect bread for fall. And some of River Grove's customers would appreciate the organic whole wheat I'd ordered for them.

While the wheat biga loaves rose, I'd bake the brioche, some of which Beck would chop, dip and fry up for French toast fingers.

After the loaves were done, I'd bake the cranberry orange scones, now cut and wrapped up in the freezer. Last would be the cinnamon rolls and the beignets. They needed to be fresh. I'd roll the cinnamon roll dough out, slather it with cinnamon sugar, butter and caramel, let it have a short rise, then get the rolls into the oven, so they'd have that just-made taste and intoxicating smell when customers came in.

Beck would cut and fry the beignet dough, then she'd get the coffee area ready for opening. This past summer, I'd given Beck expanded hours and promoted her to assistant manager of The Laughing Loaf. Because Beck now did much of the cleaning and setup the night before, our morning routine was easier, and we were more prepared to deal with anything unexpected that might come up. It so often did—whether that was a fridge malfunction, or Mayor C arriving at the back door at 6 a.m. with an urgent demand to talk.

Beck and I had worked together now for a year and a half, and we knew how each other worked. We'd settled into a comfortable routine before our morning opening. Beck, who hadn't had any work experience before The Laughing Loaf, had become a confident baker and loved to invent things. Many of her creations, like the beignets and the French toast sticks, were now on our menu.

Beck came in this morning at 5:30 a.m., with her usual basket of eggs from her chickens. She set down the basket and pulled her gloves off, her cheeks pink from the cold.

"Why does this fall have to be the absolute opposite of our summer?" She sighed. "Just a few months ago it was scorching hot in here, and now it's freezing cold. I just want *something* in between."

I smirked. "Remember how bad prep was for the concert dinners we boxed up last summer? We were drowning in sweat. Just when we get the AC installed in here, we don't need it anymore."

"Coffee?" She asked, preparing to head for the espresso machine.

"Of course," I replied as I pulled trays of brioche out of the oven with two gloved hands. "I got busy and didn't get to make any." Plunging myself into my routine this morning kept me from thinking about last night's candy-eating prowler. Or the fact that Nate was thousands of miles away. His flight had left Quito, Ecuador, at this point, en route to the Galapagos Islands. Not that I was keeping track or anything.

This would be a test for us. We'd seen each other most days since we'd met earlier this year. After my experience with Ben, I did a lot of thinking. Did I need a man in my life? If the week passed without missing him, I told myself, wouldn't that mean that we *weren't* supposed to be together?

I'd have to see whether that would make me feel relieved or heartbroken, and I didn't feel like slowing down for that right now.

The brioche loaves—i.e., our best advertising for the bakery—filled the back room with a rich, buttery sweet aroma. Every time I saw them on the cooling racks, I was tempted to plunge a hand into one of the perfectly smooth golden-brown loaves and pull off a hunk. There was only one thing that kept me from doing this—we needed each one of those loaves. All of them would be sold to eager customers or sliced up into French toast sticks by Beck.

Before we opened the doors at 7, I set the joke of the day on its stand on the counter.

Laughing Loaf Joke of the Day
An apple a day keeps the doctor away.
At least if you throw it hard enough.

When the high schoolers came in, the joke got more laughs than groans, so I claimed it as a personal victory.

At 8:30, the chief and the mayor came in and did their usual meeting. They seemed to be discussing traffic through town again. They had a map spread out on the table between them. Mayor C was using a pencil to tap on different areas of the map, and then the chief would either nod or shake his head.

During our slow time, I went back to baking loaves. As I shaped the fragrant whole wheat raisin biga loaves, my mind scrolled through the many things on my mind. I remembered something the agents had said at their visit last month.

We have a contact close by who is keeping an eye out 24/7 for anything suspicious in town.

I hadn't thought much about that when I'd heard it. Other than I was relieved, as it seemed like the agents were taking my fears seriously. Now I wondered. What did that mean? Did that mean there was someone here in our area who was working for the marshals, keeping an eye on things, on people and on us? If so, who was it? Was it someone I knew and interacted with?

I shaped the loaves, then pressed down lightly as I turned them with my hands, until they became tight and compact. I dusted each of the bannetons with flour and set the balls of dough in their place for the last rise.

Then I took out the biga and added the remaining ingredients to the sticky brown dough: molasses, raisins and chopped walnuts. The smell was rich and deep, and brought back memories of making bread in high school in the wet, cold early mornings in Seattle. I couldn't wait to smell the loaves baking.

I took two big trays of cinnamon rolls out of the oven

and went up front to check on the line and see if Beck needed help. She was busy at the espresso machine, making up a big order for someone I hadn't seen in the bakery before. A middle-aged man in a Stanford sweatshirt.

"Welcome to the The Laughing Loaf." I moved toward the display case. "Can I get you any pastries today?"

"I've heard good things about your cinnamon rolls," he smiled. "And your brioche. Can I get four cinnamon rolls and a brioche loaf? My wife and kids and I are on our way down to Monterey to the aquarium. We read the article about your bakery and thought we should check it out on our way."

"*The Mercury News* article?" I tried to keep a smile on my face as fear bounced around in my chest. This is what Beck had mentioned. I hoped my name didn't appear in the article.

He took out his phone. He scrolled through a few screens and stopped. "It had tips for places to check out on the weekend. Ah, here it is." He reached across the counter to show me.

Hidden Treasure in the Santa Cruz Mountains: The Laughing Loaf Bakery

Take winding Highway 9 through the mountains on your way to Santa Cruz to check out the Laughing Loaf Bakery – a gem in the small town of River Grove. Cinnamon rolls, scones of new and surprising flavors, a clever joke of the day, and a cheery barista who will renew your faith in mankind.

There was a photo of Beck with a huge smile on her face, holding out a latte over the counter embellished with her best latte design: a multi-layered heart.

I scrolled through to the end. The article was short. It didn't mention my name, only Beck's. Relief sweat flooded my body, as Beck set the man's four coffees into a drinks carrier.

"This is nice to see," I told the man, as I went to wrap up the cinnamon rolls. "Thanks for showing me."

"No problem." He smiled as he slipped his phone into his pocket. "I can tell from the smell of that bread baking, I won't be disappointed."

I handed him the boxed cinnamon rolls. "We've got brioche loaves just coming out now. If I wrap up a loaf for you, please promise you won't dig into it for another hour. It'll be better if you wait for it to cool."

The man's face turned up in a grin and held up crossed fingers. "We will try our best."

I double-bagged the warm bread and handed it to him. He slid his card into the pay station.

The man put his card away and handed the bread and cinnamon rolls to his teenaged son, standing behind him.

"Have a great day at the Aquarium!" Beck called out from the espresso machine.

The man and his son waved and left for their car, parked out front.

I didn't have time to dissolve into fear or celebrate the news of The Laughing Loaf's new fame. There was a growing line in front of our counter. I saw mostly townies: Jake Daniels in for Speed Spot's morning coffee order, Eric and Annie Morton in for their regular coffee and a loaf of brioche, and a few more locals. Beck and I kept busy bagging pastries and bread. We made espresso drinks for the next half hour without much of a break.

Afterwards, I went into the back room for some relief.

Maybe I should just accept this newfound notoriety for the bakery and celebrate that we were potentially getting a new crop of customers from out of town. But somewhere down inside, I felt the fear return.

Laughing Loaf was on the map.

I hoped I was not.

Chapter Five

t lunch, when business had tapered off, I left Beck in charge and prepared to take Biga for a walk.

I strapped on Biga's harness and snapped the leash onto it. My idea was to walk down the trail, following the river toward our house. I wanted to follow the path the prowler had taken last night. Not that I didn't trust that Deputy Brad Castro had done a thorough job in his search for the prowler. I had to see the prowler's escape route for myself.

My previous job had involved problem-solving, and I'd found that I had to do some fact-finding before I approached a problem. Today I had to see where the prowler had gone, and Biga would get a nice walk in the bargain. A win for everybody.

Biga was beside himself with joy at the prospect of a walk. After we went out the back door of the bakery, he bounded down the steps, pulling me with him.

The crisp air smelled like fall, wood smoke from chimneys mingled with the most enticing smell on earth: someone cooking bacon. We headed for the rough dirt trail along the river, crunching over fallen leaves and brown pine needles. We hadn't had a lot of rain this year yet, so the river had narrowed, with more dry, exposed bank visible on its edges. California always seemed to teeter on the verge of a drought. I hoped that a good amount of rain would come this winter, so we wouldn't be in danger of water rationing.

As we walked, I tried to imagine the prowler running down the path. Judging from what I'd heard, he or she had gotten into a car and pulled away. The most likely spots for that would be Great Branch Way, about 500 feet ahead of us, or the next outlet to the San Luciano River – Cannes Drive. The name made it sound like a posh location on the French Riviera, when in fact there wasn't much of a beach there, and it certainly wasn't posh.

After Biga stopped to do his business about five times, we arrived at Great Branch Way, a big cul-de-sac that turned off from the highway. There were three houses at its end, where it abutted the river. There was the Morton's house, fairly new, built by Eric Morton's construction company. It was an imitation craftsman-style home with wood-shingle siding, and it looked newer and more upscale than most of the houses in River Grove. Its large windows, surrounded by bright white shutters, looked out to the river. Annie Morton was in front of the house, trying to wrangle Pixie into the house.

"Hey, Annie!" I called to her.

When Biga turned in that direction and saw Pixie, his eyes narrowed. He growled and began barking with all the intensity his twelve pounds could muster, straining at his leash. *So, my adversary, we meet again.*

Pixie sat motionless, looking back at Biga, as this indignant little dog yipped at him. Under his sheaf of fluffy hair, Pixie's eyes looked genuinely puzzled at my dog's reaction.

I shrugged and laughed. "Biga's ready to go at it. Sorry about that."

Annie Morton rubbed her dog's head affectionately. "At least Pixie's calmed down now and maybe I can get him in the house. Out for a lunchtime walk? I love this weather."

"Me, too." I thought about asking Annie if she'd heard anything last night around dinner time. If the prowler had been on the trail, the Mortons might have heard something.

"We had a prowler last night near our front porch." I watched as Biga sniffed around and finally chose a small clump of weeds to do his business on. "He took off on the trail. We had Brad Castro out to take a look. Did you guys hear anything last night around dinner time?"

Annie's brown eyes widened. "Someone snooping around your house? That's scary, Gracie." She looked down for a moment, thinking. "Wait a minute. Pixie started barking after we finished dinner. I mean, he often does that when he sees a squirrel out the window. He stood by the front door, growling for about five minutes."

"Did you see anyone along the river?" The Mortons' kitchen and dining area looked out onto the river, so it would be possible at that time to see someone on the trail, even in the dark.

Annie shook her head, as Pixie lumbered good-naturedly up the stairs to the porch. "I didn't. I think Eric would have said something if he did. I can ask when I talk to him later and get back to you."

"I appreciate that, Annie." Biga was getting bored now, having thoroughly explored every bush and plant in the Mortons' yard. He was pulling on the leash to continue down the trail, so I said my goodbyes to Annie and we continued in the direction of the "beach."

I inhaled the cold, moist air. The river had a deep,

earthy scent today. Leaves from the deciduous trees had fallen on the riverbank, decomposing into mulch. The air felt damp, as if rain was on its way. It was almost a Pacific Northwest day, reminding me of my life in Seattle. I noticed with surprise though, this time the memory no longer made me feel as sad.

We were nearing Cannes Way, where the trees opened up in a clearing, revealing a narrow strip of sandy rocky soil along the river. It wasn't the kind of smooth sandy beach you'd see down in Santa Cruz, but I'd seen parents and kids hanging out here before, parents sitting in camp chairs as their kids splashed happily in the water, especially in the summer, when the river was the closest place to get relief from the heat.

The street was pocked with potholes and not as well kept up as Great Branch. The fragmented pavement ended abruptly, just short of the trail, in a clump of mud, rocks and concrete chunks. There were a couple of rundown houses on Cannes Way, one of which had had a For Sale sign on it for as long as we'd lived in River Grove.

The wind blew from across the river, cold and wet, and I shivered. Biga tugged on the leash. Even he wanted to move on.

I stopped on the trail and looked toward the street. There were footprints in the half-dried mud, and they looked like they'd been left by someone wearing heeled boots, not the athletic shoes people typically wore in River Grove. I took out my phone and snapped a couple of pictures. This might be something to show Brad Castro.

Biga was sniffing around the prints. Then he growled.

When I looked down, I saw something halfway buried in the mud. A small square of white and grey. I dug into the half-dried mud until I pulled it out. My throat tightened when I turned it over.

It was a grainy black-and-white photo.

Of my bakery.

With GRACIE MARKLEY and the address written on the back.

Chapter Six

I brushed the mud off the edges. It was a candid shot of the front of The Laughing Loaf, with a sign on the door advertising our Fall Spice Latte, so it was recent. I'd only had the sign up since the beginning of September.

Nausea turned in my stomach. First the letter, now a photo of my bakery with my name on it. Unlike the letter I'd received with the Russian stamp, it had my current name. Mostly. *Grace* was the name everyone had called me in Seattle. Nobody called me that here. To everyone in River Grove, I was *Gracie.* WITSEC recommends that you choose a name close to your given first name, because it's so rooted in people to respond to it.

I stepped back from my escalating fear for a moment as I thought about the possibilities. There was the Mercury News's short blurb about the bakery a few weeks ago. Maybe someone had stopped by and taken a photo to pass on to someone. *This is the place where I got those delicious beignets.* But why would they have written my name on it?

Who printed photos these days? If someone was giving a recommendation to someone else, they'd snap a photo on their phone and pass it on via a text message or email. Also would someone take a photo with a 35mm camera, have it developed, and hand it to someone? That was pretty old school. I wasn't an expert in spy equipment or at police stakeouts. But this seemed like some kind of surveillance photo.

I wanted to tell Agents LaValle and Piccelli.

But I had to do it carefully and unobserved. There were special procedures for this. I took Biga back to the bakery, led him into his pen, and gave him a treat.

At 2:30 p.m., I told Beck I wanted to make some adjustments to the walnut raisin biga recipe, and that I'd be here for a while. I also wanted to do some reorganizing in the back room. I'd close up the bakery myself.

"Oh. Okay." Beck looked disappointed. I know she liked to use the time after closing to play with her baking ideas. Giving her free reign to experiment had definitely benefited the bakery.

"I had something I was going to work on." Then she brightened. "But that's okay. I can do it at home."

I smiled at her. "I'm excited to see what you've been tinkering with."

"Can I grab some of the apples you brought in?" She looked over at the bag of apples I'd bought from an orchard over in Gilroy last week.

"Of course." She pulled her wicker basket out from under one of the baking tables and went over to take some apples. She turned a few over in her hands, trying to pick the best ones. "Now you're making me curious, Beck. What are you working on?"

Beck raised her eyebrows and gave me a mysterious smile as she loaded up the basket and covered it. As she prepared to leave, she grinned. "I may bring something in tomorrow. I need to work on it a little more. We'll see."

Much as I loved Beck, I sighed with relief when she exited the back door of the bakery.

I waited a few minutes, making sure she hadn't forgotten anything and needed to come back—because that had happened many times before.

I was on my way to unlock the burner phone I used to call the marshals when my cell phone rang. The ring tone I used for my friend Elana. I admit, I wanted to ignore it and plow through to my call to the marshals. But Elana had been a good friend to me.

"Hey, Elana, what's up?

"I left work early and need to blow off some steam," she said, her voice hoarse. She sniffed. "The bakery's closed now, right? Can I stop by for a quick chat?"

"Sure, come on over. Park in the alley. I'll let you in the back."

Fifteen minutes later, Elana tapped on the back door.

When I opened the door and saw her face, I knew she'd been crying.

"Hey, come on in." I hugged her. "Is it time for me to break out the emergency zinfandel?"

Elana smiled weakly and shook her head. She wiped at her eyes with a tissue. "Naw, it's okay. But thanks."

I took a bottle of cold water out of the fridge and handed it to her.

"Let's talk in the dining area."

We sat at the corner table, usually occupied by Mayor C and the chief, for their top-secret morning strategy meetings. No one could see the table from the large front windows.

"What's up? Talk to me, El."

She flipped the cap of the water bottle open and took a gulp of water.

"Work's been horrible since my promotion back in February." She started in. "It started out okay, but as soon as I took on the full load of responsibilities, I saw the backlog of paperwork and projects. I'm convinced the person before me must have done absolutely nothing. I've been sorting through files over the past six months, trying to organize and fix as much as I can. Now I'm getting yelled at for things not being done and for the things he promised to do—but never did. My boss doesn't get why it's taking me so long to get up to speed. The VP she reports to doesn't either."

"Do they have any idea how incompetent this guy was?"

Elana wiped her eyes and took another gulp of water. She shook her head.

"He's a schmoozer and gets away with it because he hangs out with a lot of the VPs."

"I'm sorry, Elana." I touched her arm. "That sucks."

She swallowed and wiped her eyes. "When I talk to Kirk about it, he tells me to suck it up. That I should approach my boss and be direct and upfront, document everything this guy didn't get done. With office politics, it's not that simple." She pressed her lips together. "Last night, I told Kirk I wanted to quit."

Seeing my friend's desperation made me wonder if I'd gotten so wrapped up in my problems, I hadn't noticed how bad things had gotten for Elana.

"What did Kirk say?"

"He told me he thought I could handle this and that quitting would be running away. He said I should try not to get so *emotional* about it."

"Whoa." I let out a long sigh and shook my head. "Oh, Kirk."

"Now I don't even want to be around him, Gracie. He was giving me all this advice, but it was what *he'd* do as a CEO, in his company, not my situation at all. I need him to hear me." She began crying again. "I don't think I've ever felt this way. Incompetent."

"You *are* competent. Are you kidding me?" Elana was one of the strongest, most capable women I knew. "Just because your predecessor was a jerk and left you to clean up his mistakes, doesn't mean you're incompetent. Just because your husband told you to suck it up, doesn't mean that you should."

Elana sniffed again. "I need to tell Kirk that. Tell him to shut up and just listen. I need his support."

I nodded. "You do. You had no idea what you were getting into when you took on this job."

"Thanks, Gracie." She took another gulp from the water bottle. "I needed to talk to someone. I'm glad it was you."

Her comment touched me. I gave her a hug and saw her to the back door.

"Hey, how are you doing with Nate off on his shoot?" She looked up at me. "I'm sorry—he left yesterday, didn't he?"

"Yep. I'm fine." I shrugged. "It's only been one day."

After she left, I went into Biga's pen and played with him for a few minutes, then decided I should do what I intended to do: call the agents and tell them what I'd found on my walk with Biga.

My heart pounding, I moved through the bakery, from the front to the back, checking everything in the dining area, my tiny office, the back room, and the storeroom, where Nate's ten-speed leaned up against the wall, awaiting his return. At the sight of the bike, the memory of that airport kiss sent a giddy feeling through me.

I looked out the back door into the alley, just to be sure, then locked and bolted the door.

I sat down in my chair, at the desk in my tiny office. I ran my hand over the large drawer in my desk and opened a smooth panel attached to its bottom. I felt for the key and curled my fingers around it. I reached around my computer display to unlock a compartment on the desk.

I pulled out a slim burner phone, which had only one use: to contact the agents. I tapped the preset for the number. I last used it when I'd gotten the letter back in July.

The phone rang twice.

"Hello, Gracie. Piccelli here." Her stern, throaty voice had an urgency to it, as if she'd been waiting for this moment to be called into action. I pictured her answering the call in her ruffly yellow sundress, and even though I was nervous, I wanted to laugh.

I told her about the person snooping on our property, then about the photo I'd found in the mud. My voice began to shake.

"Would anybody else have a reason to take a photo of your bakery?"

I could tell she wasn't taking the photo as seriously as the prowler issue.

I told her about the article in *The Mercury News*, and the fact that it had included Beck's name.

"The bakery photo was taken in the past month. You can see a sign on the door advertising our fall latte." I knew there wasn't anyone around, but I kept my voice low, the level of a whisper. "The photo doesn't look like something a newspaper would use for a story. It's really grainy. It looks like it was taken with—" I scrambled for the word, thinking of the equipment Nate used when we were out in the woods and he wanted to capture a bird high up in the trees. "A telephoto lens."

"You're thinking the person taking it was a distance away and zoomed in to take the photo," Piccelli said.

"Yes. I guess."

"This isn't setting off any alarms for me yet," Piccelli said. "There could be a number of reasons someone could have taken this picture. Anyone could have done it. And the fact that the article on The Laughing Loaf came out in *The Merc* recently opens things up even further. So people like your bakery. You've gotten some good publicity and word of mouth. Congratulations, Gracie. You're doing better after relocation than 99 percent of the witnesses in the program. I can tell you some crazy stories of WITSEC fails."

"Yeah, but coming so soon after the prowler," I said insistently. "And the letter. Someone out there who knows who we are and where we are. They know where my father and I live, and they know where I work. It's making me anxious."

Was I being overdramatic? I tried to look at things through Piccelli's eyes. The photo could have been from the newspaper. The prowler could have been someone out for a walk or someone who was trying to ask us for directions. I'd gone after him with my flashlight, screamed, and scared the heck out of him.

On the other hand, maybe the prowler *had* been sent by a foreign government. Maybe he'd even come to the bakery. I'd try to ask Beck about anyone who'd come into the bakery recently who looked out of place, maybe even foreign. I'd have to be careful about how I brought it up.

Piccelli was silent for a while. I heard clicks on a keyboard in the background.

"Gracie, I'm going to check in again with our local

contact. I'll relay this information. Trust me in this, we've got you covered. Remember, we've never—"

"—lost a witness," I finished for her, and let out a quiet sigh of exasperation. I'd heard this from both agents, but it certainly didn't make me feel safer in my current situation.

I tried to think of who the local contact could be. Was it someone I knew?

"Can you tell me who this local person is? It would be helpful to know."

Piccelli cleared her throat. "There are reasons I can't reveal that. Believe me, Gracie. We've got a system set up and it works." She paused for a moment. "If for some reason, this does escalate, we can move you to a placement somewhere else. We can do that quickly. There's no need to worry."

After we ended the call, I placed the phone in its compartment behind my computer and slid the key back into its slot in my desk drawer. I slumped down in my chair and stared blankly at my computer screen. The brioche wafted its sweet buttery goodness in from the back room, and I smelled the yeasty, earthy scent of dough, as the whole wheat biga loaves began their overnight rise. Their rich scent wasn't bringing me any comfort. I felt worse now than before I made the call.

Earlier this year, I'd finally started to relax. I felt at home here, part of this quirky, friendly community. I thought my days of turmoil had ended and I'd been given the chance to restart my life.

If these events were connected with my testimony against Ben and his network, then my father, Biga, and I would have to move. Leave River Grove and everyone we cared about in this little community. I'd close or sell the bakery. Beck would have to leave a job she loved.

I'd have to leave Nate behind, with no explanation. Or at least a lame, made-up one.

My throat felt tight, clogged with unshed tears.

For the first time in months, I felt happy. Grounded.

Now it could all be ending.

Chapter Seven

That night I had one thing going for me.

All I'd have to do for dinner was pull it out of the fridge and put it in the oven: Shepherd's Pie, a casserole of ground lamb and vegetables, topped with a fluffy, cheesy covering of mashed potatoes. I'd mixed it up last night. Running a bakery was teaching me the value of prepping in advance.

I'd made it to my dad's specifications. It was a dish he'd grown up eating, and I'd made it very light on spice, just this side of bland, which he'd love. He wouldn't have to drink milk to wash it down or pick anything offensive out of it. He'd come a long way in his ability and willingness to make dinner, so this was kind of a reward. The way his eyes lit up when he saw the familiar casserole was priceless.

As I quickly added lots of salt and pepper to the portion on my own plate, I told him what I'd found in the mud and about my call to Piccelli. He was the only person I could talk to this about. It was such a relief to talk about it openly with somebody.

"I felt like she was brushing me off," I said, after I made quick progress on my casserole portion. "She seemed to think there was some other explanation for the photo."

I could tell my professor father was carefully preparing his answer; the gears and levers were engaging in his head, judging by the slight frown on his forehead and the knitted eyebrows.

"Ockham's Razor, put forth by William of Ockham, says the simpler explanation of a situation is preferred and more likely to be true." He dabbed the corner of his mouth with his napkin. "The newspaper came out and took photos at The Laughing Loaf, isn't that true?"

I nodded reluctantly and swallowed a bite of mashed potatoes, mentally patting myself on the back for how creamy and delicious they were. "They published a photo of Beck and one of her lattes. It scared me at first. But it was great publicity for us. It's already bringing in customers."

"The simplest explanation is that the photographer took a photo of the bakery. Or maybe the reporter was given that photo by someone at the newspaper to show what the bakery looked like."

I didn't want to acknowledge his point, but he was right. "But as a *younger* person, it seems more likely to me that someone would have taken a photo on their phone and texted it to the reporter to show him or her what the bakery looks like."

My dad took a drink of wine and fingered the glass's stem as he thought about this. "I'm suggesting that you're piecing together an argument that these events are related, when in fact they may be completely unrelated."

"But our visitor from the other night, the photo, and the letter. All of these took place within three months." I pushed my empty plate away. "If these things are related, and someone's out to get revenge for my testimony, we could be in danger. LaValle and Piccelli said that letter addressed to me was a threat."

"But the marshals are not concerned." My father said tentatively, almost as if it were a question.

"Piccelli isn't." I stood up and began stacking our dishes. "She talked again about that local contact who's keeping an eye out for us. I'd like to know who it is. She wouldn't tell me anything. It's probably somebody we don't know."

I was anxious and thinking about this all too much. My father was oblivious, fully trusting in the marshals to protect us and our identities. I wondered if the truth was somewhere in between the two of us.

After I cleared the table, my father immediately got up and started rinsing dishes and loading the dishwasher. Relieved that he'd started cleaning up before drifting off to his physics readings, I relaxed with Biga for a while on the couch while checking emails and text messages on my phone.

When Biga needed to go outside to do his business, I let him out into the fenced backyard and stood in the doorway. A small creature was making its way along the fence, and I looked for the telltale white stripe. The last thing I needed was for Biga to start a fight with a skunk.

The night seemed darker than usual. It was damp and misty, the kind of weather that seeps uncomfortably into your bones. Biga poked around the big yard so long, I was starting to get cold with the door open.

I shivered and pulled my sweater around me. I heard the river rushing beyond the fence and, in the distance, the sounds of a car rolling down the highway into town.

I was so focused on trying to track my little dog in the dark yard that I jumped when my phone vibrated in my hand.

I'd just received another text. But it wasn't Elana this time.

It's officially lights out here in the camp.
Got time to talk?

So much for not missing him yet. The relief and joy that washed over me when I read the message completely transformed my mood.

Yes! Let me get my dog back in the house.

I called Biga, and he scampered up the back steps into the house. With all the drama and intensity of a teenaged girl, I bounded into my room, shut the door, and flopped stomach first onto my bed to talk to—*my boyfriend.*

OK, I'm here.

I managed to let the phone go through one full ring before I picked up.

"Gracie. I can't talk too loudly since I've got roommates here. We're an hour ahead of you. I wanted to hear your voice," Nate said softly. His voice sounded crystal-clear despite the fact that he was more than three thousand miles away and on an isolated island. "How are things in River Grove?"

I couldn't tell him about the biggest thing on my mind, as much as I wanted to.

"Not bad," I started in, trying to be upbeat. "There was

an article in *The Mercury News* about The Laughing Loaf. As a weekend recommendation for good places to eat off the beaten path. We had a family come in today on their way to Monterey to check us out."

"That's great, Gracie. And well deserved." I could hear his smile over the phone. "How is that early morning opening working out for you?"

I laughed. "Well, I'm dead meat by about 2 p.m.. It's a long workday. But I have to say, starting the morning with a bakery full of teenagers is very energizing."

I heard the deep rumble of Nate's laugh. "And loud, I'm sure."

"No kidding."

Nate told me about his first day on the shoot, which consisted of capturing photos of one particular species of finch in its natural habitat. He described taking hundreds of photos, at different settings and angles, while the bird was flying and while it was eating seeds.

"I fell off a cliff trying to get this one bird. I had it all lined up—perfect angle to catch his beak and eyes, nice backdrop of the blue sky. Then the bird hopped up to a higher rock and started pecking at a seed pod, which was even a better shot. I tried to move quickly and quietly to get closer. I pivoted and put my foot down behind me and realized there was nothing under it—"

"You fell off a cliff?" I gasped. "Are you okay?"

Nate laughed. "I've got some scrapes and bruises, but I'm fine. It was just an eight-foot drop. Those people who make bad decisions to take selfies at the edge of the Grand Canyon are more relatable to me now."

I pictured him, looking buff on the rugged cliffs of the islands. I'd love to have one of those selfies myself, but I wasn't going to ask for one. But there was something I could ask about.

"Hey, I had a random question about photography." That wasn't revealing anything I wasn't supposed to tell. Piccelli didn't even think the photo was important.

"Okay—shoot." He cracked up at his own camera pun, while I groaned.

"This is going to sound strange," I said, prefacing it. "I was hiking down the river trail when I found a small black-and-white photo buried in the mud. It was a print of the front of the bakery, and it was recent."

"Okay." Nate said. "Could be some kid's assignment for a photography class at River Grove High. You've seen those kids running around downtown taking photos of everything after school." He had a point. The teenagers liked to take photos downtown for class, and I'd had a few kids ask to take photos of the back room for their projects.

"Someone wrote my *name* on the back of the photo, which feels a little stalker-y. The quality was grainy. I was wondering if it could have been taken with one of those big lenses you use when you're taking photos of birds far away —like you used with the blue heron nests up in the trees."

"A telephoto lens? That could explain the graininess." Nate was quiet for a moment. "Gracie, I know you like to look into things around town. Please, will you be careful? I appreciate that you did that on my brother's behalf, but that's also a way to make enemies."

I already had some pretty big enemies.

We talked a little more about what Nate was planning to shoot tomorrow, then the frequency of my yawns increased as he got into the zoological classifications and detailed physical features of each of the birds. He was a bird nerd in his happy place, but I had to get up at 3:45 a.m. We said goodbye, and Nate said he'd try to text tomorrow night.

I heard familiar scratching on my door—Biga trying to get into my room. I groaned.

That meant I had to get up off the bed. I got up and let him in, went to brush my teeth, then staggered back to my bed, where I promptly collapsed.

Chapter Eight

With the help of a 20-ounce latte, I was wide awake and ready to prep for early opening at 4:30 am the next morning.

The first hint that it was going to be a difficult day was the fact that the women's restroom door jammed shut. I was relieved that it didn't do this when I was inside it—but I'd be needing it again, especially after drinking all that coffee.

When I came out and closed it, the door wouldn't open, no matter what I did to it. The ancient wooden door, which had been repainted recently, tended to get stuck when the weather turned damp—the downside of owning a beautiful, hundred-year-old building. But it was not a good turn of events, since we'd have fifteen young women in the bakery in less than an hour.

I tried running a good strong knife along the edge of the door near the door knob, which stripped off some of the paint but didn't unstick the door.

"Let me see if Sam's left home yet." Beck pulled her phone out of her apron pocket to call her husband, who was a cabinet installer for Silicon Valley home renovations. "He's got tools and fixes these things all the time."

In fifteen minutes, Sam came in the back door, tool chest with him. Within a few minutes, he'd taken off the doorknob assembly and gotten the door open. He used a planer to sand down the edge of the door, so it would freely open and close. No one would be trapped inside. I let out a sigh of relief as I saw time ticking down to our opening.

To thank him, I made a goodie basket of cinnamon rolls and beignets, and Beck made him a latte with a happy faced heart.

We opened the doors at 7 a.m., to more teenagers than I'd ever seen come into the bakery. And they were talking as loudly and furiously as stockbrokers on a Wall Street trading floor. They poured in, backpacks in hand, and took over nearly every table in the dining area. This could be a problem if they didn't all clear out by the time the rest of the town came in around 8.

Whatever good feelings lingered from Nate's call last night faded as I realized this was going to be a hard morning. Sometimes it just works out that way — as if it's nearing the end of the month and there's some official quota of bad events that needs to be met. So the bad things start piling up, one after the other.

At 7:30, at the height of the teenaged chaos, Beck came to me as I was loading the display case with a fresh batch of cinnamon rolls.

"We're out of French toast sticks, Gracie." She whispered. "*Everyone* wants them, and we've got more high schoolers than I planned for. I used all the brioche I cut."

"Didn't you try regular biga bread when you were testing the recipe?" I asked. "Try that. Or I could harsh their mellow by telling them we're out of French toast sticks for the day."

She bit her lip and thought about it. "I've done a few experiments. I know what I can add to the egg mixture. I think I can slice, dip and fry up the regular bread pretty quickly. Can you cover the espresso machine?"

"Go for it." I nodded and finished loading up the baked goods, while Beck hurried to the back to make more sticks. Then I dashed to the back room to slide a large tray of cranberry orange scones into the oven.

Amid the flurry of voices and snapping of three-ring binders, I swore I heard a high-pitched whine somewhere in the distance. It sounded like a siren.

The kids were noisy today, gabbing back and forth across the tables excitedly. Two young men, whom I knew for a fact were seniors and should have known better, were looking over at the girls and pushing each other as they whispered. Out of the corner of my eye, I could see things escalating as I made espresso drinks.

Soon I heard the noise of a large, full, paper cup hitting the floor. I turned and saw brown liquid splattering over a good ten-square feet of the dining room floor.

"Jeb, you big dweeb."

"Just stop, Sky. You knocked it when you shoved me. It wasn't my fault."

After handing Chloe Westerman her hazelnut latte over the counter, I walked over to the table.

"From what I saw, you're both responsible," I stood over the two very tall, lanky seniors, frowning. A look of fear crossed their faces. As soon as they stood up, their heights would change the balance of power.

"See the cart where you bus dishes? There are towels in

the bin. If you both clean up the mess, you can stay till it's time to leave for school. If not, you can leave now."

The two looked at me dumbfounded for a few seconds, then looked in the direction of the girls. Finally, they pushed their chairs back and sauntered over to the cart. One of them went back to pick up the cup and throw it away, while the other grabbed two damp towels. They both squatted down and sopped up the liquid on the floor.

"There's too much," the taller of the two, Sky, said in a whiny voice, holding a dripping towel in one hand. "I can't get it all."

I went to pull the bin off the bussing cart and set it on the floor. "It's not that hard, guys. Squeeze the towel out in here and keep going."

I heard a chorus of *ooooooooooh* coming from the big round table. The girls had watched this interaction, giggling among themselves. When I shot them a stern look, they quickly went back to their homework. Within five minutes, the two young men had wiped the floor, which was still damp, but much cleaner.

Beck came out with the French toast sticks, which smelled just as amazing as the ones made with the brioche—maybe even better. A sweet, spicy aroma hung in the air. She slid the tray into the display case and immediately a line formed at the counter.

"I think they came out okay," she said with a shy smile. She reached down to the showcase with the tongs and pulled out a couple of golden-brown sticks, setting them on a plate with a syrup cup. "See what you think, Gracie."

I dipped a stick in the cup and took a bite. Then I tried to figure out what she'd added to the coating. I could pick out vanilla, ginger, cinnamon and even orange zest. "These flavors are so good. You need to keep making these, Beck."

"Thanks, Gracie."

Her cheeks blushing pink, Beck returned to her post at the espresso machine. I started filling clamshell containers with the sticks and the cups of dipping syrup. I must have filled six or seven orders when I started smelling something. A sharp smell, like burning fruit.

The scones!

In my rush to take over on the espresso machine, I'd forgotten to set a timer.

"Just a moment. I'll be right back," I told the young woman next in line.

I rushed to the back room, slid on silicone mitts, and pulled the tray out of the oven. The scones had started to smoke. Their tops were dark brown, speckled with blackened cranberries. While Biga would be very happy to gnaw on one, they were beyond saving. The acrid smell permeated the room and would soon drift out into the dining area of the bakery. I took the tray out the back entrance and set it on top of a metal trash bin in the alley for now.

As I ran back into the bakery, I tried to remember the last time I'd burned something. There were more trays of cut scones in the freezer, but it seemed like such a waste to lose one.

The high schoolers finally straggled out at 8:15, caffeinated and full of breakfast. Chloe Westerman slung her backpack over her shoulder and came up to the counter on her way out.

"Gracie, you were right to call out Jeb and Sky this morning. It was hilarious watching them clean up. They've been bickering at school. They both got early acceptance from their colleges. They're so full of themselves." She rolled her eyes as she turned to leave. "Seniors."

The next wave, adult River Grovians, began lining up at

the counter. The noise level had decreased dramatically. As usual, I took orders and Beck made drinks. I'd had time to put in another tray of scones and carried the hand timer in the pocket of my apron, so thankfully, fresh scones were ready for the new crowd.

Jake Daniels of Speed Spot Motors leaned over, a hand on the counter, scanning the showcase.

"Gracie, Aiden says those French Toast things are really good. Can you give me a couple boxes to take to the shop?" Aiden Franzi, a kid who'd gotten into some trouble earlier in the year, was now employed after school at Speed Spot. Aiden's mother was a single parent and had suffered a series of health problems. I was happy to see that Jake and his wife Jeanne had stepped in to mentor Aiden and serve as his second family.

"You got it." I handed him the two clamshells.

With current customers taken care of, I made the rounds, tidying the dining area and collecting cups and plates left behind. Beck went to the back room to fry up more beignets. I'd finally started to relax after this morning's onslaught. I wondered if it had really been worth it to open up early for the high school crowd. Sure, it brought in good business, and in general, I liked the kids. But if this many kids, this loud, came in every school morning? I didn't think I could handle it.

I went to the back room to see if Beck had more beignets, since we'd gotten down to a half dozen in the case. And Chief Westerman hadn't even come in yet.

Beck stood by the stove, her phone in her hand. Her face looked strangely pale. She pressed her lips together and looked at me with troubled eyes.

I ran to her and hugged her.

"Beck, what's wrong? Tell me." She swallowed hard and turned off the bubbling pot of oil.

Sirens wailed loudly in the direction of the highway.

"Sam just called. He was on Highway 9 driving in to work, when he saw someone by the side of the road. He pulled over and ran out to help him."

She stared at her phone, her eyes bleary.

"It was a man in an overcoat, dead. Sam said it looks like somebody shot him."

Chapter Nine

Beck was especially sensitive to anyone or anything being hurt. I got her to sit down. Thankfully, things had slowed down at the bakery.

"Is Sam going on to work or will he be coming back to town?" I asked, as I brought Beck her bright pink water bottle.

"He's talking to the chief and Brad." She opened the bottle and took a gulp. "He says he'll be answering questions for a while. He needs to get to his site to do an installation today, so he can't come back."

I peered out into the dining area to check on things. No one was at the counter. A few people sat at tables, calmly chatting and drinking their coffee. A mom was pulling off pieces of her cinnamon roll and feeding them to her toddler, who squirmed in a booster seat strapped to a chair.

I wondered who the man in the overcoat was. Was he someone from River Grove—or an outsider? Maybe as my dad had said, I was trying to connect unrelated events, but the prowler had worn a long coat. I wanted to talk to the chief and Brad to get more information. They were probably still down by the highway, investigating the scene and trying to sort things out.

I didn't expect to see the chief and Mayor C in the bakery today, not for their regular morning chat anyway. They'd been coming in around 8:30-9 a.m. every morning to get their breakfast and to talk about public safety in River Grove. As a team, they were secretive and almost comically puffed up with their own sense of power. But they both cared about the town, and they seemed to have a genuine friendship. This past summer when they'd stopped talking to each other, I was surprised at how out of sorts it made me feel.

Beck's phone rang, and she quickly jumped up and reached for it on the table. "It's Sam."

I heard the bell on the front door ring, and I knew I needed to be up front dealing with customers. I signaled to Beck that I'd take care of the front. She nodded and continued listening to Sam.

Mayor C looked like a Lego person in her bright yellow down jacket and black jeans. She was at the front counter, talking on her phone.

"Tell me as soon as you hear something, Dave. Gotcha. Ping me when you get back in town."

She ended the call and leaned on the counter.

"Good morning, Gracie." She looked over at the case. "I'll have a kale frittata cup and a latte, with oat milk, of course."

"Large?" I asked. My guess is that if River Grove had just had another murder, she'd need a large today. Not long ago, the mayor and the chief had proudly declared the town's crime wave was over.

She let out a heavy sigh. "Please, Gracie."

"A body was found out on the highway this morning.

My theory is that it's no one from around here. It certainly didn't look like it, from what Dave said. The perps must have killed him somewhere else and dumped him on the highway."

Mayor C, who'd grown up in River Grove, saw our small town and the rest of Northern California as *us* and *them*.

"Sam told Beck he was wearing an overcoat. What did he look like?" I remembered Brad's comment that the prowler might have been wearing heeled boots.

"He said the man looked like he was in his twenties." Mayor C looked me over like a county fair livestock judge assessing a heifer. "Younger than you."

I was surprised she was willingly telling me all this. I put it down to the fact that we'd bonded during the summer's murder case. The victim, musician Noah Thornton Bell, had been her closest friend in high school and beyond. I'd helped her out during that time, and maybe it had built her trust in me.

As I talked to the mayor, I saw Beck emerge from the back room, still pale. She passed behind me and made her way to the espresso machine.

"You said large latte with oat milk, Mayor C?" Beck asked as cheerily as she could in her current state.

I went to the case and pulled out a frittata cup with the tongs and put it on a plate.

"Corinne, if you need anything, let me know," I said as I handed it to her. "It must be hard for you to go through this, after what happened with Noah last summer."

Apparently, I'd pushed it with my show of concern. Mayor C raised an eyebrow and her face scrunched up in a look of annoyance. She picked up her latte and plate.

"I'm just fine, Gracie. After all, this stranger isn't *my* problem."

* * *

A little before noon, as I wiped down tables, I watched Chief Dave Westerman park his big old Crown Victoria River Grove PD car on the street and head for his office in city hall, which years ago had been Meyer's hardware store. The chief opened the green-painted door and hurried inside.

Not like I was trying to keep an eye on his movements, but River Grove City Hall was right across from The Laughing Loaf. I saw the comings and goings without trying to. It was convenient to have the police so close by, as I'd seen when someone threw a rock through the bakery's front window earlier this year. Deputy Brad literally ran across the street to respond.

Thoughts were spinning through my head, and I wanted so badly to know who the man in the overcoat was. I was uncomfortable with not knowing who had snooped around our house and who'd taken the photo of my bakery. Wouldn't it be nice to know that the source of all the last three months' uneasiness was no longer a threat?

I kept myself busy by mixing up a new batch of whole-wheat walnut raisin loaves. I mixed the pre-ferment in the large plastic tub, inhaling the earthy scent of the rich whole wheat flour as I mixed in warm water and a small amount of yeast and made a thick, sticky paste. Whole wheat works best, in my opinion, when it's combined with regular bread flour. It tastes better, rises higher, and makes for a lighter crumb: the look of the bread when you slice it, with its holes and texture. I'd leave the pre-ferment to proof until early tomorrow morning, when I mix in bread flour, yeast, molasses and chopped walnuts.

Then I made a batch of lemon blueberry scones, part of which I'd bake tomorrow. The rest I'd freeze for daily baking. It made things so much easier to have frozen, cut scones on hand, which I could pop in the oven when I needed them.

As I wrapped the scones for the freezer, I heard Beck talking to a customer.

When I realized it was the chief, I washed and dried my hands and headed for the counter.

"Good afternoon, chief, how is your day going?" I figured it was better if I acted as if I hadn't heard of the body on the highway. Or at least didn't bring it up right away.

The chief gave me an odd look, while he continued talking to Beck.

"Your husband was very helpful, Mrs. Rodriguez," he nodded. "He stayed with us on the highway for over an hour, answering questions. He said he would have stayed longer to help, but he had to get to San Jose for work. Sam's a good man."

Beck smiled shyly as she put his latte down on the counter, along with a bag of the last of the beignets we had.

"He *is* a good man," I agreed, as I remembered how cheerfully Sam had pitched in to help with the bathroom door this morning and the bakery's front window when it was smashed earlier this year. "Chief, would you like me to warm these beignets up for you?"

The chief shook his head. "They'll be fine."

After picking up his latte and grabbing the bag, the chief turned to me, a frown on his face.

"I need a word with you, Gracie." He looked around the dining area and focused on a table in the back. "In private."

Was the chief going to ask me to help with this case? He'd done that with the Noah Bell case in the summer when he and Mayor C weren't on speaking terms and he'd lost his partner in crime.

When we were seated at the back table in the dining area, he looked around at the nearly deserted dining area first. My first clue that this was serious was that he hadn't even touched his bag of beignets. He set a manila envelope on the table between us. He lowered his voice.

"The body wasn't anyone we know in town. We found no ID on him. No personal effects."

I felt the beginnings of nausea in my stomach as the chief sat back in his chair and crossed his arms. Judging from his body language and tone, something was off.

"There was one thing we found on him, Gracie." He raised his eyebrows as he pulled a photo print from the manila envelope and set it down in front of me. He'd snapped a picture of a small square photo.

"He had this picture of you in his coat pocket."

Chapter Ten

My hands started to shake, like they had the night I'd seen the prowler head for our porch.

The photo was a color photo of me smiling. My hair was pulled back in a ponytail. It looked like it had been taken outdoors, a distance away, a little like the one of the bakery. But I wasn't sure this one was taken in River Grove.

It hit me now. A virtual line of string stretched between the man I'd chased down the trail, to the photo of the bakery I'd found in the mud, to this body on the highway.

My mental police murder board.

The square photo of me was a similar size as the one of the bakery. The man I chased down the trail was wearing a long coat.

"You okay, Gracie?" The chief watched me closely, studying my face. As if he suspected I had something to do with the man's death. I took a deep breath.

"I need you to look at the man and tell me if you know him." The chief pulled another large photo out of the envelope and set it in front of me.

My first emotion was shock; he looked young, as young as the two out-of-control high school seniors who spilled the coffee this morning. He was thin, with sharp features and short, blond hair. His steel blue eyes were wide open, as if something had startled him. He wore a grey-green overcoat.

Somewhere inside, I heard a tiny, nagging voice. *You've seen this person.*

It could be that he had a certain look, like a type. Maybe he resembled someone I knew.

I shook my head. "I don't."

"Gracie." The chief looked me over. "Is there anything you need to tell me?"

"No, other than it scares me that there's been another murder in town. And that this guy had my picture in his pocket."

I was stumped. If this was the man who'd been trying to track me down, who had killed *him*?

"You heard about our prowler a few days ago," I said, trying to remember anything I'd seen of the man as I'd chased him in the dark. I had to be careful what I said to the chief. If it turned out Overcoat Man was some foreign spy, and he was the man on our property, people might wonder why this had happened to *us*. And start asking questions.

"Brad didn't find anyone when he checked it out," the chief said gruffly, dismissing the incident with a shake of his head. "So there were footprints. And candy wrappers anyone could have dropped. Your house isn't that far off the trail. Have you thought maybe the guy had just gotten lost? Maybe he was just coming up to your porch to ask for help."

For the first time, I reflected on the past three months and had a thought.

The letter in my mailbox had been terrifying. What if

in my shock at seeing my old name, I'd started looking at everything suspiciously?

For some people, that might qualify as a paranoid episode. In my defense, it could actually happen to me—foreign powers threatened to come after me because of my court testimony. That was why my father and I were in witness protection.

"I guess that's possible," I said slowly. I still needed to tell LaValle and Piccelli about the body found on the highway. Maybe they already knew.

"The mayor and I believe this death could be an isolated incident," the chief said, finally opening his bag of beignets. "We think he was dumped there after being shot somewhere else—with an assault rifle. He's a John Doe right now. The county is asking the public for help in identifying him. The fact that he had your picture in his pocket is—well, it's our *only* clue." He took a bite of beignet, without taking his eyes off me.

I raised my eyebrows and let out a heavy sigh. I couldn't say anything about my past life, even to local law enforcement. I'd been grilled about this in WITSEC orientation and by Piccelli and LaValle.

"You have no idea why this man would have your photo?

I thought about my answer. "No. Other than maybe he was a stalker."

"Well, you don't have to worry about him now." The chief said grimly, scrutinizing my face. Judging by the look on his face, he either suspected I was involved in the man's death or he was trying to protect me. "Do you and your father own a gun?"

"We don't," I said emphatically. The thought of my

scholarly father toting a gun made me want to laugh. "I can't imagine either of us using one."

The chief was now on his second beignet. Powdered sugar now dusted his moustache.

"Gracie, I recommend you be careful, especially at night—and in the early morning when you come to the bakery."

"I'll be careful, chief. I usually have my watchdog with me." I relaxed a little, relieved that he wasn't asking any more uncomfortable questions about my connection with Overcoat Man. "He wouldn't be much good in fighting off an attacker, but he's got the most annoying bark I know."

Chapter Eleven

Again, I told Beck I'd be staying late and closing up.

After today, I was exhausted, but I wanted to talk to the marshals about the body on the highway. And the photo in his pocket.

I didn't push Beck out right away after we closed the doors. She'd been peeling apples and blending dough for crust. She was in the zone, fixated on testing her latest recipe. I wondered if this was her escape from the troubling call from Sam this morning. Like me, baking was a source of comfort for her.

While I mixed a new batch of whole wheat biga, she pressed tart dough into six small tins. I watched her progress with interest as she carefully laid apple slices in the tins.

Minutes later she opened the oven and pulled out a tray of small, personal-sized tarts, with apple slices neatly set in spirals. The warm cinnamon apple scent, combined with the buttery crust and a hint of caramel, was irresistible.

They looked a little like French *tartes* but smelled like

good old fashioned apple pie. These would round out our fall offerings, and the smell of them promised to be as good an advertisement for the bakery as the brioche.

She lay the tray on the metal table and looked at them critically. "I think I've got the recipe down now."

"You want a taste?" I hadn't had lunch and the smell of these was making my stomach rumble.

She grinned. "After they cool, I'll plate one up for you."

My assistant manager didn't like to brag, but if she admitted something was good, it was usually *very* good.

"How do *you* feel about them, Beck?"

"I think I've got it down. They're spicy and a little bit tart, a little bit sweet. I'm happy with the crust." She bent over the tarts with a loving look in her eyes, which communicated more than her words. "I think—well, they're pretty good."

"They're beautiful," I said. "A few years ago, I went to Paris and ate something that looked just like one of these, in an outdoor café."

Ben and I had spent our honeymoon in Paris. I'd been dizzy with the beauty of the city—the food, the music, the art. And in love with the idea of being married to Ben, a handsome, brilliant man—the man of my dreams as far as I knew. Little did I know that I'd just made the biggest mistake of my life.

Beck's voice broke into my thoughts, and I snapped back to reality.

"And the tarts are something you could bake the afternoon before," she said excitedly.

Beck was right. We had a lot that had to be baked in the morning, so I was always looking to optimize our oven space.

"You're not only creative, but you're also practical." I nodded. "That will be a big help."

With everything wiped down and set for the morning crowd, which I hoped was less chaotic than today's, I went back to the desk in my tiny office to check the day's receipts. We were doing a lot more business since we'd started opening early, but I still wondered if the morning noise and craziness was worth it.

Beck brought me a tart on a plate with a fork and looked at me expectantly.

I took a bite. Buttery crust, cinnamon-y apples with just enough firmness and a nice tang to them. I closed my eyes and savored the bite.

"Well done, Beck," I said after I'd swallowed. "I'd like to introduce them soon. We'll need to find a source for the apples and order anything extra we'll need for these." I immediately took two more bites. Food is one of the quickest ways to get to my happy place. And despite today's troubling events, the tart was cheering me up.

"How about next week?"

I thought about that as I finished chewing. "We can do that. Let's start soon with a small batch or two, to make sure we can fit them into our baking schedule. And of course, to build up demand. People will get here and see they're sold out."

Beck was glowing. "Thank you for letting me do my experiments. If I was working somewhere else, I wouldn't have the freedom to create new things."

I laughed. "Beck, seriously. Your experiments are good for business."

After Beck left, I went through the bakery and locked front and back doors, after making sure everyone was out. I even checked the restrooms and the storeroom. Once I was sure I was alone, I felt for the key compartment in my drawer and slid it open to get the key. Then I unlocked my burner phone from the compartment behind my monitor.

LaValle answered this time. I was hoping he'd be more sympathetic and that the marshals would take my concerns seriously.

"Gracie, we heard about the body found on the highway."

My heart pounded. "Did you know he had a photo of me in his pocket?"

"Wait a minute." LaValle's tone was sharp. "I didn't hear about any photo."

"Our police chief showed me. He responded when Sam Rodriguez called it in and he snapped a picture of it on his phone." Then it dawned on me. If the marshals didn't know about the photo, it was possible the chief hadn't made his find public. Had Chief Westerman been trying to protect me?

"Piccelli told me about the photo of the bakery you found. She thought it was probably related to the story in *The Mercury News*." He was quiet for a moment. "But this changes things."

While I was glad he was validating my fears, his serious tone made me more worried.

"Do you have any idea who this man was?" I asked. "If he was a foreign agent, wouldn't you have heard something from your intelligence channels? Or maybe other agencies?"

"We're circulating a photo of the body. We ran it through image identification software but we haven't had any plausible hits yet."

"If he was an agent coming after me and he was killed by someone else—does that mean my father and I aren't in danger anymore?" I was frustrated and I heard it coming out in my tone.

LaValle grunted. "If this man was a threat to you and your father for the takedown of the spy network, someone got to him before he got to you. But we need to be careful. Whoever sent him will probably send a replacement." He paused for a moment. "On the other hand, if he was your stalker for other reasons—well—"

I supposed he could have been a stalker, but it wouldn't be high on my list of possibilities.

I swallowed. "He looked like a kid. A teenager. Regardless of what his intentions were, I can't feel good about him being killed."

I remembered his startled face from the photo the chief had shown me. His mouth open and his big blue eyes widened in fear.

Who was he? I couldn't be open with the chief about my situation. I wasn't sure I could get help from the marshals—or from this mysterious local contact they told me was keeping an eye on us.

LaValle left me with a promise that he'd find answers as to who Overcoat Man was and what he was doing with my photo. But I was skeptical. I also wondered if the chief planned to reveal to anyone else that it was me in the photo.

It might be up to me to find out why the man was here and who had killed him.

Chapter Twelve

I'd had the presence of mind at 4 a.m. that morning to set up chicken and white bean chili in the crockpot and put a timer on it—and to leave Biga at home.

When I finally came through the door at 5 p.m., I was comforted by the savory smell of chili and the loving attentions of my little dog, who frisked me for bread crumbs then put his paws on my leg. I picked him up.

My father and I started in on our steaming bowls of chili as I told him about my day. My father had heard about the body from Mary Jo.

"Do you think he was an agent trying to track you down?" My father asked as he slathered a thick slice of sourdough bread with butter. "I don't like the idea that someone was taking pictures of you."

I grimaced. "Think of how *I* feel. It's creepy." I took a heaping spoonful of the chili, fragrant with a mild chili verde sauce, and felt warmth flooding through me. "The thing is, he looked young enough to be a student at River Grove High. When I saw his face, he looked a little familiar to me."

"Maybe someone who'd come into the bakery?" He paused to talk then continued eating his bread slice.

"I still don't know if it was something I imagined. For all I know he was someone I'd seen on a TV show. Agent LaValle couldn't tell me much more than I already knew from Chief Westerman. There was no ID on him. Either someone had taken it, or the man hadn't wanted to be identified."

My father scraped the last bits of his soup from the bowl and sat back in his chair.

"It's possible someone killed him, and we don't need to worry anymore." As usual, my father was much more optimistic about this than I was. "Maybe it was a counterintelligence agent, who'd been on their trail."

I shook my head. "The marshals would know about this. LaValle seemed completely puzzled as to Overcoat Man's identity. I could tell this took him by surprise."

That stumped my father. Biga jumped up onto his lap, and he scratched the dog's back. Biga turned over to bare his stomach for more scratching.

Should I tell my father about what Piccelli had said about relocating us quickly if it looked like we were being hunted? There were too many things up in the air now. I didn't know—and the agents didn't seem to know—if we were in danger.

"Dad, when I talked to Piccelli a couple days ago, she said that if it looked like our identity had been compromised and we were in danger, they'd relocate us somewhere else."

He looked at me, his face turning pale. "We'd leave River Grove?"

"If it looked like we were in danger." I looked down at my bowl. I was losing my appetite. "They've done it with other witnesses, and she said they know how to do it quickly. We could be moved overnight."

His mouth turned down and his eyes looked moist. "So I wouldn't even be able to say goodbye to Mary Jo." I judged by my dad's reaction, that things were still on with him and his lady friend, who ran the plant nursery, Growing Affection, at the outskirts of town. They seemed to have an off-and-on relationship.

I sighed. "We couldn't tell anyone. I couldn't tell Nate. As much as we care about these people in our lives, somebody could let something slip."

I still carried guilt for what I'd done to us two years ago —which had prompted my father and I to relocate. As my physics professor father often told me, life is a series of causes and effects. My conscience told me that I needed to turn Ben in; in fact, after I found the record of the foreign payments he'd received, I had to go to the authorities. If Ben was eventually exposed by someone else, I could be arrested for complicity and my father's reputation and academic position would be ruined.

I'd turned him in and testified. But that had its effect. Now it looked like we'd be on the run, under new identities, for the rest of our lives.

As much as I had my doubts about whether Mary Jo was the best option for my dad, I had no say in the matter. She wasn't my mother, who'd died when I was fifteen; in fact, she was *nothing* like the quiet, elegant Caroline Hollis, but I told myself that was okay. Mary Jo made my dad happy, most of the time anyway. And after almost eighteen years on his own, my father deserved some happiness.

I gave my father the night off and cleaned up dishes myself. It felt good to do something that produced immediate results, since I couldn't seem to make progress in my personal situation.

After dinner I went into my room with my laptop, Biga following me. I lay on the bed, googling news stories about the body found on Highway 9. I read every account of how and where the body was found.

I clicked on a local television station news video.

Can You Identify This Man?
Shooting Victim On Highway 9

An interview with Sam Rodriguez, a dazed look in his eyes, as he described seeing something on the side of the highway and pulling over. An interview with Chief Westerman, who speculated that the man had been killed somewhere else and dumped on the side of the road.

The reporter held the microphone out to the chief.

"Chief, do you have any speculation on who this person could be? You're saying there's no ID on him."

The chief frowned and looked back at the side of the road. He shook his head. "Unfortunately, there was no ID, no personal belongings or anything on him by which we can identify him."

I stopped the video.

Wait a minute.

The chief didn't mention a photo. Had he chosen not to tell reporters there was a photo?

Why would he do this? Did he know more about my past than he let on? I began to wonder if he knew about, or if he *was*, the local contact the marshals had mentioned. I had a hard time thinking of the chief as a federal agent. And if he was, wouldn't he have told the agents he found the photo? LaValle didn't mention it.

I did some more googling, trying to see if there were any missing person reports of a young man, maybe even a teenager—tall, thin, blond hair. The chief had researched this using better databases, but I thought I'd see what came up.

I scrolled through photos from all over the US, even some from Canada. None of the young men looked quite like the photo the chief had shown me. There were a few that looked close, but there was something that didn't match up on each. One had a soft baby face instead of Overcoat Man's sharp features. Another was tall, maybe 6 feet 2, but he was muscular, not thin and wiry.

Who had this person been? If he'd been the one making his way to my front porch that night, what had he intended to do?

Around 8:30, I let Biga out for his last run around the backyard. He took forever, sniffing and cycling through the bushes in the yard. He barked ferociously at a small shadow making its way across the yard. I hoped and prayed it was not a skunk. Annie Morton had told me of Pixie's encounter with a skunk a few days ago and all the baths they'd given the big dog to rid him of the smell. I certainly didn't want that smell in my house; it apparently lasted for days, even after multiple baths.

Nate and I were supposed to talk tonight, so I thought about how I'd tell the story. I had to tell him about the murder, but there was so much I had to edit out of the discussion. The photo in Overcoat Man's pocket. My fears that this young man had been sent by a foreign government —to spy on me or to do worse. And of course, about my fears that me, Biga, and my father would have to leave River Grove very soon.

Was it fair to have a relationship with someone who

didn't know all this? I couldn't fully be myself with Nate. I couldn't tell him about my fears. He could never know my real name or what I'd been through with Ben. I went back to the idea that Nate's time away could be a good time to evaluate whether being with him was worth the risk. I couldn't say I didn't miss him.

But I did think about him. I couldn't wait for his calls at night, and he'd only been gone three days.

As I went back inside with Biga, my phone lit up with a text.

> Got time to talk?

I hesitated. I waited till Biga was comfortably curled up on my father's lap in his lounger. I got a glass of water, then walked slowly back to my room, and set it down on my nightstand. I plumped my pillow up and lay against it, then wrapped my arms around my knees.

I looked down at my phone on the nightstand. The text glowed back at me. It didn't seem to want to go away.

What if I ghosted him? What if I didn't respond?

If I did that, I could eliminate at least one complication in my crazy life. I wouldn't have to second guess everything I said, worry that I'd let something slip. I wouldn't have to feel guilty that I was propping up a façade, not being myself with someone who had been genuine, vulnerable even, with me over the past eight months.

I could prepare myself emotionally for what could be a quick departure from River Grove. I had no guarantee we'd still be here when Nate returned from the Galapagos.

My heart pounded. I thought of Nate's blue eyes, and remembered the way he reached out to me, his big hand wrapping around mine like a warm, safe glove, as he pulled me up on one of the river rocks to sit with him on our evening walks. I remember the strong electricity of my hand in his.

I looked down at my phone, paralyzed.

Then watched, helpless, as a new text popped up.

You've had a long day. You must be asleep.
No worries, Gracie. Talk to you soon.

Chapter Thirteen

I tossed and turned in bed that night, feeling guilty about ghosting Nate.

And trying to figure out why the chief hadn't told the truth about finding my photo.

After dragging myself out of bed at 4 a.m., I showered and got dressed, then went to pull a clean apron out of my dryer. Biga followed me around the house, determined that I wasn't going to leave without him. I put him in the crate, and we went out to the car to head downtown.

I turned on all the lights in the bakery and put on a playlist of the goofiest 80s tunes I could find to put me in a better mood. Once Biga was settled in his pen with water and food, I went to work.

As the speakers blared out "Karma Chameleon" by Culture Club, I sang along as I mixed flour, molasses and raisins into the tub of pre-ferment for the whole wheat walnut raisin bread. The Italian bread method called *biga*, which I'd named my dog in honor of, was one of my favorite doughs. A pre-ferment that you set up the day before, it's versatile and low maintenance. You get some of the depth of flavor you get with sourdough without having to maintain a starter—though I also kept and replenished a tub of that, too.

After my conflicting thoughts about Nate last night, the earthy smell of the whole wheat dough comforted me. It felt good to be up to my elbows in sweet, warm, sticky dough. I put the tub back into the proofer for a three-hour rise, then went to work mixing brioche dough. I set it up for a slow overnight rise in the industrial fridge. These loaves would not be baked until we came in tomorrow morning. Rising slowly in colder temperatures deepens the flavor of the bread.

Since we still had a good supply of eggs from Beck's chickens. I took out a dozen and a half to make the rich, yellow brioche dough, knowing there would still be enough for the kale tarragon cups which Beck would mix up when she came in. I didn't rely solely on the eggs she brought in, but they tasted so much better than what I could buy wholesale. Beck brought them in, excited to share, because that's the kind of person she was. I sneaked compensation into Beck's paycheck for them, not wanting to take advantage of her generosity.

Beck came in at 5:30, obviously feeling better after the trauma of yesterday's murder. She hummed along to the music as she went to work on putting together the frittata mixture. She chopped fragrant herbs and fresh kale and blended them into the beaten eggs, along with grated cheddar.

"Today's got to be a better day," Beck said, as she pulled out the tart tins and lined them up on a baking sheet. She took tart crust dough and began pressing it into a tin. "After I do these, I'll get the French Toast Sticks going. I cut a lot of extra bread and have some white biga loaves cut up just in case. We should be fine today for the students."

"Loud teenagers, murder and burned scones. We can only go up from there." I rolled my eyes as I pulled trays of frozen, cut scones from the freezer now that the oven was up to temperature. "I'm going to lay down the law for any high schooler who acts up. I'm hoping we don't have quite as many today. It's nice to have the business, and I really *do* like teenagers, but yesterday was crazy. I'm wondering if I need to set a time limit for them, to make sure they're all cleared out by the time everyone else comes in."

"But Gracie, you handled the situation with the two seniors really well," Beck said as she pressed dough into a tart tin. "You made an example of them in front of the other students. That might solve the problem, more than any rule you could set up."

That seemed to fit with what Chloe Westerman said yesterday. "You could be right. If I remember what I was like as a teenager, my first response to rules was to try to get around them."

Beck laughed. "I can't picture you doing that. You seem like a pretty good rule follower to me. But I remember that's what my brothers did. It must be a teenage thing." Beck had five brothers. Since I'd grown up an only child, I couldn't even imagine what that had been like for her.

There was something I wanted to ask her, since Overcoat Man had been on my mind all day.

"Beck, I'd like to talk to Sam about finding the man on the highway. Would you and Sam be okay if I came over and chatted with him?"

Beck's black eyes brightened. "I was hoping you'd be doing some of your snooping around to figure out what happened. Sam's been really down about what he saw. He's frustrated that they can't even identify the man."

"Maybe I can come over tonight." I asked. "Would that work?"

"I know." Beck got a sudden inspiration. "What if you and your father come over for dinner? I know it's late notice, but Sam and I would love to have you. I'll make dinner. And—" She had a mysterious smile on her face. "—a surprise dessert."

How could I refuse that?

Unless my father had a hot date with Mary Jo Hartman tonight, he'd probably be happy to enjoy Beck's cooking.

"Would it be okay to bring Biga?" I asked. "As long as he can't see your chickens outside, he'll be fine."

"Perfect, Gracie." She clasped her hands together in excitement. "I'll see you and your dad at 6."

We opened at 7 a.m. to a quieter, smaller bunch of high schoolers. They staked out spots at the tables with bags and backpacks, then lined up to order. Over the next half hour, more came into the bakery, but the students already sitting quietly doing their homework must have had an influence on the students coming in. The newcomers looked around, read the room, and took their seats without disruption.

At 7:45, I turned to Beck and let out a big sigh of relief. She came up to me and gave me a high five.

As my father liked to say, maybe yesterday's early morning chaos was just "a statistical aberration."

Mayor C and the chief made their way in during the exodus of high schoolers, grim looks on their faces. Mayor C did the ordering, while the chief sat down at the corner table and began writing furiously on a legal tablet. The next time I looked his way, he'd picked up his phone and was talking in low tones.

"Good morning, Corinne," I nodded at the mayor as I pulled a frittata for her and three beignets for the chief out of the display case. "Anything new on the murder yesterday?" I wondered if the chief had told her about the photo he'd found.

"No identification still." The mayor shook her head as she peeled off her gloves and shoved them into the pocket of her bright yellow down jacket. She picked up her oat milk latte and took a sip. "The chief has a theory that the man wasn't from around here. That he might have been a foreigner."

My heart jumped up to my throat and began pounding.

"What makes him think that?" I said as casually as I could.

"Well, nobody here or in the state seems able to identify him." The mayor shrugged. "We knew he wasn't from River Grove, but it's looking like he's still a mystery man. The chief and I are working on the few leads he has."

I nodded as I passed the chief's Cherry Orchard Latte to the mayor.

"I'm sure River Grove's crime fighting duo will come up with something."

"Right." The mayor gave me an odd look as she fitted the two cups into a carrier and turned to head to the corner table. "Thanks, Gracie."

I watched them hunched over the table, talking in hushed tones. Today I'd try to get the chief alone.

If he had a reason for keeping that photo of me a secret, I wanted to know what it was.

· · ·

The morning brought a steady stream of customers, so Beck and I didn't get much of a break. There were the usual suspects from the downtown businesses—Jake Daniels and his wife, Jeanne, and Cheryl from the Cut and Curl. Peter James Jordan, Attorney at Law, came in his three-piece suit and flat top haircut, asking for his usual *lat-tay,* as he called it. The man seemed like he was still living in another era. He'd been unfamiliar with the drink until he'd had it for the first time at The Laughing Loaf earlier this year.

A couple of grey-haired older women in windbreakers and fanny packs came up to the counter. They were somewhere in their seventies or maybe eighties and looked like they were out on a hiking expedition.

"Good morning, ladies." I managed to say it cheerfully, though I wasn't feeling it at this point. "What can I get you?"

"We read about you in *The Mercury News,*" the shorter woman in the blue windbreaker said. "We drove up from Santa Cruz. I hear you have good beignets. You don't see those much around here." She nodded to her friend. "I'm Audrey. My friend Loretta here grew up near New Orleans and got all excited when she read that you made them here. We'll take four to go."

"Glad you came up to see us." I smiled at the two ladies. "Beck, over here on the espresso machine, makes them herself. Can I get you any drinks?"

"I'll have a large drip coffee, dear," Audrey said, while the other woman, Loretta approached the counter. "And a large spice latte for me," she piped up.

I bagged up the beignets as she slid her credit card into the pay station and Beck got started on the espresso machine.

"We're meeting some friends at the redwoods at Henry

Cowell State Park." Audrey handed the bag to Loretta, who opened it, inhaled, and let out a delighted sigh. "Your bakery's not far away, and the *Sentinel* said it's worth taking a detour for." She shot a glance at Loretta, who was taking a bite out of a chocolate beignet, closing her eyes in bliss as she ate. "We were a little afraid of coming up here because of that murder on the highway yesterday. That poor young man. It's all over the news." She frowned. "But your little town seems safe enough."

I nodded. "Thank you, Audrey. We try to look out for each other here."

Once they had their drinks, the two headed out for their redwood adventure.

By the way Loretta was clutching the beignet bag, it looked like she wasn't going to share.

* * *

When we closed at 2 p.m., I left Beck to make a batch of her caramel apple tarts in preparation for a trial launch of the treats tomorrow morning. Then I locked the bakery front door and headed across the street to city hall.

As I entered the lobby, Peony Roberts, city hall receptionist, turned her head to me slowly, like one of those creepy motion-activated owl monitors. Her hair was in braids today, which gave her a quaint, old-timey look. She looked like a plucky heroine, maybe Anne of Green Gables.

"How may I help you, Gracie?" She asked in a clipped voice.

"I need to see the chief. It's really important."

Peony looked very put upon, as she usually did when she saw me.

To be fair, she was supposed to serve as a gatekeeper for

the mayor, the chief and any of the town council members using the city hall offices. I often dodged her or slipped past her, trying to talk to who I needed, because it was usually urgent. Like now.

But this time, feeling a little guilty for my past actions, I decided I would be good. Like me, Peony took her job very seriously. I would let her do her job. I would show her some respect. Despite my impatience that I could get back to the chief's office on my own much faster.

Peony slid her antique wooden desk chair back with a screech then headed back to the small offices, built in the gutted insides of the old Meyer's hardware store. Her heels made precise clicking sounds down the hall.

Before she headed back, I heard the chief bellow.

"Damn it, Peony! Let her come on back."

As I made my way down the hall, I passed Peony. She avoided my eyes and continued on her way.

As usual, the chief was leaning back, only two legs of the chair on the ground. He tapped a pen on a tablet of yellow legal paper on his lap.

"Hey, chief." I sat down in the old, uncomfortable captain's chair in front of his desk. "How's the case going?"

He frowned. "You'd think, with all the technology we have over the hill in Silicon Valley, we'd be able to figure out who this guy was. But nothing. No credible leads from the public. DNA testing may be our best bet, but that'll take time."

I shifted uncomfortably in the chair. "I wanted to ask you something, chief."

The chief's face turned pink, and he looked like he would rather do anything but answer my question.

"I watched the local news station coverage. When they interviewed you on the scene, you said there was nothing on the body, no ID, nothing that could tie him to anyone." The chief put the pad down on his desk and all four legs of the chair on the floor. "That wasn't true."

The chief cleared his throat. "I didn't tell anyone about the photo. It fell out of his pocket, and right away, I saw it was you. I grabbed it. I recorded it in the evidence log later, but that's it."

I took a deep breath. "Why?"

"Two things." He paused as if trying to figure out how to say it. He rubbed the back of his neck. "It looked like it had been taken when you weren't aware of it. And—I talked to someone who—warned me strongly that I shouldn't make it public."

My pulse began racing. *Who?*

I would think it would be someone who knew I was in witness protection. Someone who knew Overcoat Man could have been trying to track me down. Maybe this person was the local contact assigned to watch over me and my father.

Did that mean the chief *wasn't* the local contact?

"You won't tell me who told you not to make it public."

The chief shook his head, his lips pressed into a thin line. I hadn't seen this look on the chief's face before. Was it fear?

We were at an impasse. I couldn't make any assumptions about what the chief did or did not know. I couldn't tell him I was in Witness Protection, because I had to obey the rules of WITSEC drilled into my father and I in orientation two years ago. He couldn't tell me who'd warned him not to make the photo public. Neither of us was going to share any more on the subject.

I wanted to know more, since this very directly impacted me, but it wasn't going to happen.

I needed fresh air. And thinking time.

After I left city hall, I went back to the bakery to get Biga, who was beside himself with joy at the prospect of a walk. He could barely stay still for me to clip his leash onto his harness. I grabbed my down parka, and waved to Beck, who shot me a smile. She was pulling tart trays out of the oven, while on speaker phone with Sam, making plans for a get-together at his parents' house next week.

As I passed into the shadows of the redwoods along the trail, I breathed in the cool fall air, rich with damp earth, dank river smells and wood smoke. Inside me, the tiniest spark of hope flickered. The talk with the chief didn't give me any answers, but it reassured me.

Somebody was watching out for us.

Chapter Fourteen

There's a smell the redwood forest has in fall—a damp, rich scent. Fog hovers low over the forest canopy, sometimes filtering through the trees. Water condenses on the tree needles and branches and falls in gentle sporadic drops like rain. The air feels thicker, as if it's holding you close. As Biga and I walked down the trail, it felt like the forest was giving me a big, damp hug.

The trail seemed empty this afternoon. Maybe the overcast sky and chill in the air kept people away.

As Biga and I passed the back of Riverside Saloon, Reggie McFerrin, in his usual aviator sunglasses, long black ponytail and black suit, leaned over the rail of the landing of the back stairs of the music venue.

Reggie McFerrin was a local legend, a four-time mayor of River Grove. He'd founded The Riverside in the early 1980s, transforming it from a hippie commune into a popular Bay Area venue for live music.

I'd seen an old photo of the commune hanging on the wall in city hall. It showed groups of long-haired men working alongside young women in long dresses in a garden. The dilapidated wooden house in the background had since become part of The Riverside.

Reggie had to be in his late 70s, though he didn't look it. Because he lived a nocturnal life running the music venue, he slept late and didn't come out much during the day, so his skin was pale. When I first met him in The Laughing Loaf, I thought he looked like a vampire. It had taken me a while to warm up to Reggie.

Reggie talked in cryptic ways that I couldn't always decipher, yet his kindness and offbeat wisdom got through to me. I'd been skeptical when I'd first met him: why did everyone in town revere this guy? After getting to know him in my year and a half in River Grove, I understood.

"Gracie, got some time to chat?"

I smiled up at him cheerfully. "Hey, Reggie! Of course."

Reggie quickly made his way down the stairs, then led me to a bench at the foot of the slope downhill from The Riverside, overlooking the river.

Biga was a huge Reggie fan. As soon as we were seated, Biga jumped into the man's lap.

Reggie laughed and scratched Biga's belly as he talked.

"Laughing Loaf must be doing pretty well. It's always packed. Looks like you've even got out of towners coming in now."

"Yeah," I said, reluctantly. "I wasn't trying for that. We have been getting quite a few people in who read about us in the San Jose newspaper—"

Reggie nodded. "Last weekend's *Santa Cruz Sentinel* ran a recommendation."

That must have been where Audrey and Loretta, the senior hikers, had heard about The Laughing Loaf.

I sighed and looked over at Biga, who seemed oblivious as he received his belly rub.

Reggie studied my face for a while. Or at least it looked like he was. I couldn't see his eyes behind his mirrored sunglasses.

"You don't seem happy about it."

I felt the familiar fear return to me. My stomach clenched, as it usually did when I worried.

"I came here to get away from everything. River Grove is small. That's what I wanted."

Reggie laughed softly and looked down at Biga closing his eyes in bliss.

"I came here almost sixty years ago to get away from it all. Back then, River Grove was a dying lumber town in the mountains. It was *nowhere*. A bunch of us moved into an abandoned house." He gestured up at the back of The Riverside. "And what happened? I ended up starting a place for live music. Now people come to The Riverside from all over the world to hear it. That's not what I came here for, but now I love it. I'm bringing music to people. I'm happy."

It wasn't like I was particularly sad, but Reggie's words made me tear up. He couldn't know my situation. Strangers in town, like Overcoat Man, could be legitimate threats to me and my father.

He nodded as he scratched Biga. "Sometimes opportunities are given to us. You take them or you leave them. There's no guarantee any of them will last. Best to enjoy what you have while you have it." Reggie reached down to pick up a tiny, perfectly formed pinecone that had dropped on the ground. Biga gave him the side eye, miffed that the scratching had stopped.

Reggie puzzled me. How much did he know—or guess —about my situation?

"Sometimes I feel like life moves too fast." I shivered

and wrapped my parka around me. "Just as I get comfortable with the way things are, they change."

What I hated about my life now was that I didn't know how long all this would last. I didn't know how long we'd be here. I was happy the bakery was doing well, but did it have to do well because new people—possible threats to my safety—were coming into town?

I was sounding more and more like Mayor C, who was convinced that the town's crime came from bad people coming in from Silicon Valley or Santa Cruz.

Then, as he often did, Reggie asked me a question that had nothing to do with what we were talking about.

"Gracie, do you surf?"

I shook my head. "Never tried it." On trips to nearby Santa Cruz I liked to watch the surfers on their boards, looking graceful and in control as they rode waves into shore.

"I used to years ago." Reggie looked down at my dog and smiled. "I sat on the board, waiting. The surge came, and I paddled like crazy to catch up to it, to match its speed. Then I was riding it, letting it take me where it wanted to go. Once I let it, I was free. Completely free."

The look on Reggie's face as he remembered this was close to ecstasy. I would have to think more about how this related to my situation. But right now, I had a strong desire to try surfing.

I had to get back to the bakery. Biga did not look like he wanted to get off the man's lap. But I told him "down," and he jumped off the bench.

"You gave me a lot to think about, Reggie. Like you always do."

Reggie McFerrin stood up from the bench. He rose easily, not like I'd expect someone of his age to get up.

"Anytime, Gracie. Peace to you." He gave me a two-finger salute.

Biga and I bounded down the trail in the direction of The Laughing Loaf. The walk had improved both of our moods.

I looked forward to opening the back door to the warm, cinnamon smell of the tarts Beck was baking. And I decided, despite my worries about the future, I would enjoy what I had in River Grove right now: Beck's excitement at her latest creation, our dinner with her and Sam tonight, and the loud group of enthusiastic and hungry teenagers who'd be at our door bright and early.

And since we were going to Beck and Sam's, I was relieved of any dinner duties.

There was a knot in my chest as I thought of how I'd ghosted Nate. I imagined myself on a surfboard, riding the wave as it drove me where it wanted, toward the shore.

Tonight I might need to have a lively discussion about finches.

Chapter Fifteen

"Now if you had moved your pawn like *this*—"

As we drank tea and split a caramel apple tart to tide us over before dinner at Beck's, I'd agreed to play a game of chess with my father.

My father put a finger on one of my white pawns and slid it ahead one square on the chessboard, till it was next to my toppled king.

"You could have blocked my advance with this. You could have delayed checkmate by a few moves."

"But, Dad, it wouldn't have made any difference. You win every time." I laughed, as I took a bite of my half of the tart. "I was more interested in ending my misery."

"You *could* win, but you didn't want it badly enough. Most of the game is up here." My father tapped his head. "Have your moves lined up. Think of what I will most likely do and be ready to counter it." He gave me a reproachful look. "I can *always* predict what you're going to do, dear."

I rolled my eyes, as my dad angled his fork into his tart half and sliced off a bite. He savored the combination of buttery crust and spicy apple.

"This is very good, Gracie. I'll give Beck my compliments tonight."

After we finished our tarts, I'd tell my dad about my conversation with the chief today. I wanted to share my relief with someone.

"The photo of me," I started in. "The chief didn't tell anyone about it. I watched interviews with him on the news. I read the River Grove Gazette this morning. He didn't mention it at all."

That was enough to stop my dad from taking the next bite of tart. He set his fork down.

"Why would he not talk about it? Wasn't that the only thing the young man had on him?"

"The chief said he was warned by someone not to do it." I picked crumbs of tart crust off the plate with my finger and ate them. "It could have been the local contact who's monitoring us in River Grove. The one LaValle and Piccelli told us about."

"Do you have any idea who that local contact is?" My father frowned, deep in thought.

"At first I thought it was the chief. He could be putting up a good front, but the chief is easy to read. He looked worried when I asked about the local contact and shut down the conversation pretty fast. I don't think it's him."

"What about Brad Castro?" My dad said hopefully.

"I don't think he's got the discretion or the experience to do it." I tried to think of anyone else I could. "I suppose it could be—maybe someone like Mayor C."

My dad wiped his hands carefully on his napkin, then began carefully putting the chess pieces back into their velvet-lined case. "Now that makes sense. She's one tough lady. I could picture her working with the feds," he said, sounding less like a professor and more like a crime boss.

I agreed. "Corinne would be better at keeping a secret than the chief."

It was a possibility, though I realized the contact could be someone we didn't even know. "She could. Both the chief and Piccelli wouldn't tell me who the contact was. I'm not sure why it has to be a secret. But maybe WITSEC works that way. Everyone's identity is secret."

At 6:20, my dad and I got in my car and drove to the other side of town to the Rodriguez house, which was coincidentally next door to Nate's. Nate had become good friends with Sam over the past year. When I stepped out of the car, I looked over at Nate's house, which was close to the river. Nate and Sam's ongoing project was renovating the small shed next to the house, to turn it into Nate's photography studio. From what I saw, they'd made a lot of progress in the last month. The shed was now painted grey with white trim. There were new, larger windows. Outside lighting lined the perimeter of the small building, and there was some landscaping around it—rosemary and hydrangea bushes.

Beck and Sam's house glowed with light, sort of like Beck herself.

The Rodriguez house was light yellow and surrounded by rose bushes. As we pulled up to park next to Beck's vintage VW bug, I heard chickens clucking and squawking in their pen on the side of the house. I tried to keep Biga in his crate facing away from the chickens to avoid any outbursts.

I clutched a chilled bottle in a bag. Beck had told me she grew up in a home where alcohol was not allowed, so I'd erred on the safe side and brought a bottle of sparkling apple cider.

Sam met us on the porch and invited us in.

The house smelled like roast beef and potatoes, and my stomach started to rumble.

I nudged my father. "This smells like your kind of dinner, dad."

"I am very much looking forward to this," he whispered to me excitedly.

Beck took off her oven gloves and came over to give us hugs.

"I'm so glad you were able to come tonight." Beck led us to the large, polished wood table with benches in their dining room. Beck had told me that Sam had surprised her on their first anniversary by refinishing the table her family had eaten at when she was growing up. It looked like a fancy, more comfortable version of a picnic table. I pictured Beck and her five brothers as children, sitting down for breakfast, swinging their legs as they sat on the long benches.

The rooms were painted in terra cotta shades and soft pink, accented by family photos and some brightly colored prints that reminded me of murals by Diego Rivera I'd seen on a trip with Ben to Mexico City.

I handed her the chilled sparkling cider. "My favorite! Thanks, Gracie and John. Go ahead and have a seat. Dinner will be a few more minutes. I put some cheese and crackers out as hors d'oeuvres."

Sam went in to give Beck a kiss as she worked at the stove, then returned to take the bench across from us at the table.

"Sam, that must have been hard for you that morning when you found the man on the highway," I started in. "I wanted to hear you describe what you saw. Thanks for being willing to talk to me."

Sam raised his eyebrows. "Yeah, I was heading for an installation in Saratoga, and I was planning on taking the highway all the way in. I was only about a quarter of a mile past River Grove when I saw it. Something on the side of the road, like a person, sort of flopped over on his side in some leaves. I thought he'd fallen or was drunk, maybe." He shrugged. "So I pulled over and got out. When I approached him, I saw he'd been shot in the chest. And I think he'd been there a while. From that kind of a wound, I knew he was dead, but I felt his wrist for a pulse, just the same. Then I called 911."

"You didn't see anyone nearby when you stopped?" I asked. "Was there anything around him, any debris or trash. Maybe cigarette butts?"

Sam shook his head. "Just him, in his clothes and coat on the leaves. I didn't mess with his body, because I've seen crime shows and I know you're not supposed to. But I patted him to see if he had a wallet or something. I didn't see anything at all. It's like somebody cleaned everything off him."

My father cleared his throat as he entered the conversation. "Gracie says he looked very young."

Sam's eyes widened. "At first, when I saw the coat, I assumed he was an old guy. But when I saw his face, he looked like a kid. That really hit me hard. Seventeen or eighteen, maybe. Same age as my little brother. He didn't look like a runaway or a drug user. I mean, he was clean cut. His clothes looked pretty new and good quality. Like he was some kid from Saratoga or the rich suburbs in the valley."

"Did he or his clothes look unusual? Like he was maybe from another country?"

Sam thought about this, then shook his head and shrugged. "I don't think so. He looked like a kid from California to me."

I thought about Mayor C and the chief's insistence that he'd been shot somewhere else and dropped off on the highway. "Did it look like he'd been shot at that spot?"

"Hard to say." Sam thought about that. "You'd think if he'd been shot right there, you would see more blood around him. There wasn't any."

Beck walked toward us with a bowl of potatoes, our cue that we needed to set aside the murder conversation.

"Thanks for letting me grill you, Sam." I smiled across the table. "I appreciate hearing what you noticed."

Judging from Sam's sober face, recounting that morning had been difficult for him. "I want this kid's killer found, and I will do whatever I can to help."

I got up and asked Beck if I could help carry anything or pitch in to help in the kitchen.

"You're our guest, silly." She smiled and waved a hand at me dismissively. "And anyway, we're all ready. I put some meat without seasoning out for Biga," she said, gesturing to a bowl she'd placed on some newspaper in the kitchen. Even as she said it, Biga trotted over to it eagerly.

Dinner was delicious, comfort food with a twist—the roast was steeped in a peppery blend of cumin, paprika and garlic, then garnished with fresh rosemary, a combo Beck probably created herself. My father would remark to me later that the roast would have been even better if it didn't have "all those spices."

For the rest of the evening, we set aside any mention of the murder and instead talked about things we were hoping to introduce for Christmas at the bakery.

For dessert, Beck brought out pumpkin tarts, which I

think I liked even better than the caramel apple tarts—if that was even possible.

"I've been mixing up so much tart crust lately," Beck said as she laid a plate with a tart in front of each of us. "I looked around for something new to make with it. This seemed like the right filling for the season."

On the way back to our house, I thought about how Sam had described Overcoat Man—he'd been young and looked and dressed like any American kid his age. The chief seemed to be telling everyone he thought the man was from another country.

As I thought about my reactions to seeing his photo, and what I'd heard from Sam, I doubted that.

When we got home, I took Biga outside for one last opportunity to relieve himself. He roamed the dark back-yard, sniffing for intruders and hopefully not eating anything he shouldn't have. Biga had a habit of devouring things first and asking questions later.

Then I came inside and sat down on my bed. I reached over to my nightstand and picked up my phone with shaking hands. It was a little early, but for Nate on Gala-pagos time, it was an hour later, 8:30 p.m. Earlier than his usual time to chat, but I wanted to.

My thumbs whirled over the phone as I typed.

> Sorry about last night. 4 a.m. wakeup is
> killing me. Fell asleep early. Wanna talk?

Two truths and a lie.

I still felt guilty.

I hesitated after I sent the text, waiting. Realizing I could be waiting for a while, I lay back on the bed and opened my recipe binder to look for some winter bread recipes. The whole wheat raisin walnut biga was starting to catch on with customers. I wanted to have some pre-Christmas bakes lined up for December. I leafed through pages and saw Stollen, the German Christmas bread, filled with fruit and almond paste and sprinkled with powdered sugar. I snapped open the binder rings and pulled it out to take into the bakery tomorrow so I could do a test and then order ingredients.

Ten minutes later, my phone pinged.

> Just finished going thru today's shoot. I'll call you.

A couple minutes later my phone rang.

"Gracie, it feels like a month since we talked," Nate said in his low, rumbling voice, which always got to me. "I'm busy here from 6 a.m. to 9 p.m., without much of a break."

"Don't know if you've heard. A lot's been going on here, too."

"River Grove feels like another world right now. Tell me what's going on."

I told him about the body Sam found on the highway and the efforts to identify him, leaving out the part about my photo in his pocket, of course. To distract him and provide a little comic relief, I told him about the high schoolers and my day from hell. Then about the delicious tarts Beck had made.

Nice try. Nate didn't fall for the distraction.

"No word on who the man in the overcoat was?"

"Nothing so far," I said, really hoping he'd move on. "The county sheriff's involved now, too. The chief doesn't think the man is connected to anyone in River Grove." Which, in my defense, was true.

"You've got some experience with tracking down killers, Gracie. What do you think happened?"

"I don't know what to think," I said, panicking a little and making stuff up as I went along. "He looked young. Like not much older than a high schooler. Could be a runaway. I know the chief's been checking missing person lists."

"Do you think you'll get involved, Gracie?" Nate's voice sounded concerned. I could tell, the answer he wanted to hear was no.

"I'm curious about it," I said quickly. "I'm sad he's dead. But I don't have a lot of time to investigate."

Nate let out a sigh of relief, but I worried that I'd just made a promise I couldn't keep. I'd done some googling, and I'd talked to Sam. I wanted to know what the murdered man had come here to do, because it might involve me. I wanted to know who he was—and who had murdered him.

He went on to talk about his latest shoot. His team had moved to a new island, to photograph a different species of finch. His detailed descriptions of the birds calmed me down. I wanted to keep listening to his deep voice, no matter what he was saying. It wasn't about murder. It wasn't about threats from foreign agents. It was about the habits and habitats of small birds eking out an existence on a rocky island. Even if I'd never remember all the details, the affection in his voice for these persistent little creatures soothed me.

I was telling the truth when I blurted it out quickly.

"I miss you."

Then nothing.

I wondered if we'd been cut off. When you put yourself out like that, it's a bad time to hear silence on the other end.

Nate finally spoke, his voice raspy.

"Four more days. I miss you, too. I'll have a break after this. Think you could leave the bakery in Beck's hands for a few days?"

"What do you mean?"

Panic spread through my body. What was he asking?

And could I leave the bakery and trust someone else to run it? I was worried that Overcoat Man *had* been trying to track me down—and that a replacement for him was on the way. Piccelli had said they could relocate us overnight in the event of a threat. If that happened in the next week, I'd never see Nate again.

"I thought we could go away somewhere. Just you and me."

"I'd like that." I said, vaguely, since I couldn't be sure where I'd be in four days. "Let's talk about it."

After the call, my mind wanted to continue thinking about Nate's proposition to go away—and what that would be like. What it would feel like to be with him. No Biga, no dad. No bakery responsibilities to worry about.

I decided I couldn't wait.

Chapter Sixteen

In a time of stress, the morning routine at the bakery had its advantages.

Bread has a cycle of stages to it. It's an intricate dance of time. Every morning at The Laughing Loaf, multiple things had to be mixed, proofed, shaped, and baked. Because of limited proofer and oven space, everything proceeded on a tight, carefully planned schedule.

The clock was in charge. There was no fudging or negotiating for more time, and no opportunity for procrastination or laziness. Or for fretting about my current situation.

Everything had to happen at a specific time.

That morning, after leaving Biga behind, I got into the bakery earlier than usual, at 4 a.m., despite wanting to hit snooze and nab another 15 minutes in my bed. I obeyed the clock, getting the brioche set up for baking and moving the other breads on to the next stage of their production.

Meanwhile, I had scones ready to pull out of the freezer, to be baked closer to opening for freshness. I had to roll up cinnamon roll dough and cut it into rounds. Beignets were chilling in the fridge, waiting for Beck to cut and fry them. Beck would pull out the sticks of bread waiting for dipping and frying, for the high schoolers coming in.

Following the schedule kept me busy in a mindless way. Beck came in quietly at 5:30 and started to work on her tasks. I didn't have time to worry about Nate or the recent murder.

At 7 a.m., I put out the joke of the day. Maybe I'd been thinking about the chief and Mayor C's traffic plans:

Laughing Loaf Joke of the Day
Why did the stoplight turn red?
You would, too, if you had to change in the middle of the street.

I opened the doors to a group of high schoolers, mostly young women, led by Chloe Westerman, who met me at the counter, first in line. She wore a rust-colored sweater that looked either like a vintage thrift store find or like a grandma had made it. It managed to look surprisingly hip on her.

"Hazelnut latte, Beck," she waved in the direction of the espresso machine, where Beck smiled and gave her a thumbs up. "But you guys know that. Oh, and I'll take the French toast sticks."

"How are things at the Westerman house?" I asked her cordially. Chloe and her mother lived in the chief's house in the hills, and I knew they didn't always get along.

"Grandpa just dropped me off here. I can tell you, he is *not* in a good mood," she raised her finely groomed eyebrows. "That dead guy on the highway is driving him crazy. He says the sheriff's moving in on him, trying to get him to hand the case over."

I knew from what the chief and Mayor C told me, this

had been a source of conflict for years between River Grove and the county. For most small towns in the Santa Cruz Mountains, the county sheriff handled policing duties. But due to an ancient squabble between the county and the town, River Grove's original charter specified that the town would have its own police force. The chief had talked more than once about the county's attempts to intervene in River Grove where crime was concerned.

I suspected the sheriff was urging the chief to solve the highway murder case fast or hand it over. As I saw last summer with the Noah Thornton Bell case, the chief didn't respond well to giving up control. And now, apparently, he was dealing with pressure from U.S. marshals to not make my photo public.

I filled a clamshell with French toast sticks and a container of spiced syrup and handed it to Chloe.

"I talked to the chief yesterday, and he was having a hard time." I smiled sympathetically. "Hope he wraps up the case soon."

"Yeah, me, too." Chloe grimaced as she put a sleeve on her latte cup. "All he wants to do at night is watch reruns of old cop shows and drown his sorrows in Oreos and milk. And complain about the case all the time. My mom and I are so over it."

I told Beck to wait to bring out the caramel apple tarts till the high schoolers left, since I was pretty sure our second wave of customers would be more interested in them.

After the last of the high schoolers left, she brought out the tray, which she'd arranged neatly to show off the golden-brown caramel apple tarts. The cinnamon smell wafted through the shop. The tarts looked like beautiful golden-brown wheels. I put them in prime position in the showcase, in the center of the middle shelf.

Beck brought out a sign on poster board she'd made yesterday while I was meeting with the chief.

A woman in a beret sat in a café chair at a small round table, looking down with a gleeful smile at a spiraled apple tart. She'd lettered it neatly with the headline:

Tart Your Day Right
Caramel Apple Tarts – for a limited time only!

"Nicely done, Beck." I smiled after she'd carefully set it up on a stand at the top of the case. "Is that me in Paris eating a *tarte tatin?*"

She giggled. "That's exactly what I was thinking of when I drew it."

I don't know if it was the new smell wafting in with the tarts or the sign placement, but almost everyone coming in looked at those tarts and bought one.

By 9 a.m., they were gone.

Beck was ready to pull out the empty tray and return it to the back room, but I told her to leave it.

"This is where the law of supply and demand starts to work in our favor." I whispered to Beck.

When customers came in, they first glanced at the empty tray and did a double take. Then they looked up at Beck's sign.

"What's this apple tart thing?" Jake Daniels from Speed Spot Motors bent down to look at the case. "I've been seeing people eating them. You got any more in the back?"

"We just sold out, Jake." I gave him a sad smile and shook my head. "They're brand new. We'll have some more in tomorrow. They go so fast."

"Smells really good. Like apple pie. You're not making

any more later today?" He had a hopeful look in his eyes, his hands jingling change in his pockets.

"They're a limited time item." I shrugged. "Don't worry. We'll have some more tomorrow. Be sure to get here early."

Jake wheeled on his heels. "All right. I'll be back tomorrow. For today then, give me a box of those cinnamon rolls for my crew."

"You got it," I set up a square pink box and pulled eight cinnamon rolls out of the case. Before I opened the bakery, I'd debated ordering white pastry boxes with The Laughing Loaf logo. I decided against it. Why mess with tradition? Pink bakery boxes are the standard; I'm pretty sure they trigger salivation in almost everybody.

"Thanks, Gracie," Jake nodded after pulling his credit card out of the pay station. "See you tomorrow."

After he left, Beck came up behind me and tapped me on the shoulder. "You're so bad, Gracie!" She laughed as she headed for the espresso machine. "But you're a genius."

"Can you add another dozen to what you've been making this afternoon?"

"We've got three dozen apples in the storeroom," Beck said thoughtfully. "I have some pastry crust chilling, but I'll mix up another batch when I get a break. It won't take me too long."

I lowered my voice as I spoke to her. "I figure we keep the batches small, so there's always a little less than people want. We keep that up for a few weeks, then slowly ramp up if we need to. We'll get a better idea of the quantity we need to bake. Mind if I hang out this afternoon while you're making them? I want to learn how you do it, so I can pitch in when we're busy."

Beck looked excited at this prospect. "That will be fun! I'd love to teach you, Gracie."

Tonight Elana and I were meeting up at The Riverside for drinks and appetizers. The past few days had been stressful. I was looking forward to hanging out and listening to some live music. Elana and I had bonded over our love of good wine and food over the past year and a half. Earlier this year, we dug up a clue by the river and used it to solve a local mystery that had been puzzling us.

More than anyone in River Grove, even Nate, Elana pushed up against my careful boundaries. I'd come to town sure that I'd have to sacrifice friendships because of my WITSEC status. It was true I had to be careful about what I shared, and I had to stick to the backstory the marshals had written for me. But I looked for ways to be honest and share with my friend without giving away any secrets. I'd started to find a kind of rhythm within my constraints.

When I checked my phone at noon, I had a text from Elana.

> Pick you up at 7. Wear something you can dance in.

I tried to imagine how tired I'd be at 7, after being awake since 4 a.m. I wasn't the best dancer even when I wasn't tired. But I did feel like letting off some steam. We'd see how this went.

After closing, Beck and I cleaned up the dining area and coffee area, then I mixed up doughs and started the proofing processes. Beck mixed beignet dough for tomorrow morning, and I helped her peel and core apples for tarts.

"We need some music, Gracie," Beck called as she mixed lemon juice, brown sugar, and spices into the bowl of sliced apples. "Something we can sing along to."

I put on a mix of 80s and 90s hits, and Beck started blending pastry crust, pulsing flour, sugar, cinnamon and butter in the food processor, while I set out the tart pans on a baking sheet and started pressing the prepared dough into the pans. With no customers in the bakery, we sang along to Duran Duran and Wham! loudly and enthusiastically.

Reggie McFerrin had told me to enjoy what I had, even if I didn't know how long this time and place would last. I was doing that right now.

"Gracie, looking good, but the dough should be just a little thinner." Beck interrupted our singing.

After I made the tart crusts a little thinner, she showed me how to arrange the apple slices in spirals on the crust. She did it much faster than I did. I could bake good bread, and I had a decent repertoire of breads, scones and rolls, but Beck had a talent and passion for pastry. Her creations were thoughtful and beautiful.

"Ever thought of going to school for this?" I asked, as she bent down to fine-tune a spiral of slices.

Beck laughed as if I were being silly. "I'm not leaving you. Why would I work anywhere else?"

"Because you are really *good* at this. What if you went to a school where you could learn new techniques? Maybe work at a bakery in San Francisco for a while?"

Beck stood up, her cheeks pink, a look of concern on her face. "But how would I even do that? I love working here. I don't want to leave River Grove. I live here, with Sam. It wouldn't make sense to go somewhere else."

Beck had grown up here, in this small town, in a close-knit community. All of her extended family was here. This was all she knew. I changed my tactics.

"Okay then, what if you went up to the city and took a few classes at the San Francisco Baking Institute? On things you might want to learn? We'd see about giving you a few days off here or there to go to training. The Laughing Loaf could pay for it."

Beck's face started to glow. "You would do that?"

I smiled. "I would. After all, it would benefit the bakery. You'd come up with even more new ideas, new pastries we could feature. You're already doing that, but you could do it even better. Maybe you'd learn ways to streamline how we're doing things."

Soon Beck was tearing up. She swallowed. "Really?" She came around the metal table and hugged me. "I'd love that."

After we cleaned up the back room, Beck left. I walked through the bakery, remembering what the old 1920s bank building had looked like when I first toured it with the realtor. For 20 years it had been a hamburger joint, shut down almost a year before we moved to town. It was rundown, with stained formica countertops, a grill covered with generations of grease, and evidence of a rodent infestation. It was now a polished, stylish bakery and coffee shop, where River Grovians hung out and talked about homework, dogs, work, and--in the case of Mayor C and the chief--traffic and crime.

I thought of the years I'd put into monitoring tech projects and creating spreadsheets. What did any of that matter now?

Here I baked and fed people. I listened to their stories.

Now I couldn't imagine myself doing anything else.

Anywhere else.

Chapter Seventeen

Elana picked me up at 7, wearing a bright blue and green, flowing dress. She was going to make quite a spectacle dancing in it.

I'd chosen leggings and an off-the-shoulders tunic top, which with my boots made my 5'4" frame look tall and svelte. Hopefully I could dance in it without it slipping completely off me.

Biga, not having seen me all day, was clingy and sat by the door suspiciously. He gave Elana the stink eye, guessing that I would be leaving with her.

"You ladies be careful now," my father called with a smile as he started the dishwasher. "Don't drink too much and make me have to come pick you up."

"John, with all due respect, your daughter and I are in our thirties. This isn't our first rodeo." Elana smirked. "From my experience, your daughter only drinks if it's really expensive red wine. But if it does get that bad, we'll convince Reggie to let us sleep it off in one of the Riverside suites."

"I'd feel better about that." My father smiled and went

to settle himself in his recliner. "Now you girls go have a good time."

Elana and I entered the Riverside as a three-man opening band geared up for their set. The large wood-paneled and -floored room reminded me of ski lodges I'd seen in the Pacific Northwest. The entire first floor of the saloon was open, with a stage at one end, a bar on the side with windows facing the river, and a large fireplace made of river rocks.

Tables filled the rest of the cavernous space, most of them jam-packed with diners. A roar of voices filled the place, punctuated by glasses clinking and the guitarist on stage tuning his electric guitar.

There was a kitchen visible at the end, where this past summer, I'd dropped off loaves of rustic bread for a memorial dinner for hometown rockstar, Noah Thornton Bell.

I'm glad Elana had suggested the Riverside. We'd been out to various nightspots and restaurants in the mountains and in Santa Cruz, but the Riverside felt like home to me. And by that, I mean a really fun home with great music that also served great comfort food.

"A table for two," Elana nodded at the woman standing at the podium near the entrance.

"About fifteen minutes then." She gestured ahead to the bar. "You know you can sit at the bar and order appetizers with your drinks."

"That's exactly what we want." I grinned, looking to Elana for confirmation.

"Perfect. Let's do it."

I felt my body relax as we took our seats at the bar. I recognized the bartender, Drake, who'd worked the bar nearly every time I'd been to the saloon.

"Hey, Drake! What's good tonight? I want something

that's not wine." I shot a meaningful look at Elana, wanting to prove I was capable of drinking something other than red wine.

Elana smirked at me. Drake laughed, as he polished a glass. "Sure, Gracie. We've got a couple of new fall drinks. A Maple Old Fashioned if you like whiskey. Or Not Far from the Tree, which is apple brandy with citrus juice and spices."

"I'll take the Maple Old Fashioned. With chips and Reggie's guacamole. Give us a double order." Elana's eyes widened and mouthed YES. Reggie brought it to our back-yard picnic last summer, and it was the best guacamole I'd ever tasted.

"You got it." Drake nodded and went to work.

Elana scanned the drinks menu and finally settled on a chocolate martini.

Judging by her carefree attitude tonight, I wondered if things were going better with Elana's promotion from hell.

"How's the work situation? Getting any better?"

She gave me a big smile. "Good all around. Kirk finally started listening to me. My boss now understands my situation. My schmoozing predecessor is now facing the consequences of his actions. She talked to the VPs. I suspect he'll be gone on the next round of layoffs."

"Excellent." I gave her a two-handed high five. "I'm glad we're out tonight." I smiled at Drake as he went to work on our drinks. I leaned back in my chair. "I needed a break."

"Opening earlier must be killing you." She looked at me curiously. "How do you stay up past 7?"

"I'm getting used to it. Beck's coming in early and staying later, and that helps. I have a love-hate relationship with the high schoolers coming in before school. Love them when they're quiet and doing their homework, hate them when they're being loud and spilling things."

Elana shook her head. "I remember you thought a lot about that decision."

"I really do like teenagers. I love that they're hanging out at the bakery. I'm going to lay down some ground rules if they keep acting up."

Elana's eyes lit up. "Hey, what do you think of the murder on the highway this week? Sounds like the chief has made zero progress on the case."

Drake handed me my drink, and I took that moment to think about my response and to try not to show how anxious I felt.

"It sounded terrible." I swallowed my first taste of my maple Old Fashioned. It went down incredibly smoothly. "The guy looked pretty young. Just a kid."

"I can't believe they haven't identified him yet." Elana took a dainty sip of her chocolate martini. "I heard a rumor that he's from another country. Russia, maybe."

Quickly, my eyes darted her way. "Really? Where did you hear that?"

"Town gossip. Cheryl from Cut and Curl said the chief was in for a haircut. He told her he suspected it. He thinks that's why nobody's identified him yet."

I was thinking the same thing, but I wasn't going to tell her that. "Why do you think somebody from Russia would be in River Grove?"

Elana shrugged and laughed. "Maybe he was a spy? Not sure why a spy would be in the Santa Cruz mountains. Maybe somebody's trying to steal RG Pizza's prized dough recipe."

I laughed so hard I almost choked on a gulp of my drink.

The slogan on top of RG's menu said: *Our Crust Has Been a Carefully Guarded Family Secret for 30 Years.*

"I've had the pizza, and I don't think anyone would want to steal it. The only person who raves about it is Brad Castro."

The Old Fashioned was making me feel comfortably loopy, taking the edge off my nagging anxiety. When the waitress set down a basket of tortilla chips and an oversized bowl of guacamole, I felt even better. With no real dinner tonight and only nibbling at the bakery, I was hungry. I needed to eat something to balance out the strong drink. I grabbed chips and started dipping. The creamy, garlicky guacamole was amazing.

I'd just finished my drink, when the band started their set with the steady rhythmic chug of a bass, then the incredibly loud, twangy electric guitar joined in. I could barely hear Elana. She motioned to me then stood up.

"C'mon, girl! Let's dance!"

We went out to the dance floor in front of the stage, which was quickly filling up with everyone from the bar and tables. The band was a rockabilly group. It wasn't a style of music I listened to, but the three-man group played fun, danceable music. Couples did some impressive swing dance moves on the floor closest to the stage, while Elana and I danced freeform on the side with a dozen people who weren't dancing with anyone, just grooving to the music. As usual, Elana threw herself into dancing with complete abandon. I moved to the music, my mind emptied of all this week's worries.

After half a dozen songs, Elana and I stumbled back to the bar and plopped down in our seats.

"I needed that so badly." I grinned, feeling invigorated

and a little dizzy, a combination of the dancing and the drink. I felt great.

"Wait till the main act, Velvet Dogs. They come on in a half an hour," Elana looked back at the stage, where the opening band seemed to be winding down. "Kirk's seen them here before. They're supposed to be really good. We need to fortify ourselves with another drink and more guac so we can be ready."

This time I told Drake I wanted the "Not Far from the Tree" cocktail. I wanted something spicy.

A few adoring fans of the three-man band still playing swayed to the music in front of the stage as the band played a slow, Elvis-like ballad, while most of the crowd returned to their seats.

As I looked around the room, I had a weird feeling that someone was watching me. I scanned the tables, then the area around the stage to see who it could be. I didn't see anyone looking at me; most were engaged in conversation or watching the band. Then I glanced behind me at a few chairs set up in front of the stone fireplace. My eyes rested on an older man who stared back at me with intense black eyes that seemed to bore into me. He looked to be in his fifties or sixties, with short gray hair. He was wearing a black leather jacket, zipped up to his neck.

I looked away as Drake set my drink down on the bar. When I looked back at the fireplace, I saw the grey-haired man talking to someone next to him—a younger man wearing a San Francisco Giants baseball cap, a little fluff of hair under his lip, a soul patch. He looked like he was also watching me, but when I met his eyes, he lowered his head suddenly till all I could see was the San Francisco Giants logo. My heart started pounding.

There were times when I'd felt people watching me

with interest because they wanted to buy me a drink or hit on me. This felt very different. I felt like I was being monitored somehow. Tracked.

"Hey, are you okay?" said Elana, lowering her voice. She must have been watching what was going on between me and the men by the fireplace.

I turned to her and whispered. "Those men over there have been watching me for a while. Not in a good way. It's making me uncomfortable."

Elana frowned as she thought for a moment. "You focus on your drink and guac. Talk to Drake. Don't look at them, okay? I'll watch them for a while and see what they do."

I asked Drake for a glass of water. If I had to react quickly—or flee—more alcohol was a bad idea. I ate more chips and guac, if anything to get some food in me because I still felt a little dizzy.

Elana was a natural at this. She angled herself in her chair, in the direction of the men, watching them from the corner of her eye, while pretending to be absorbed in conversation with me. She talked loudly, acted slightly tipsy, and pretended to take repeated gulps of her drink. Then she gestured excitedly with her hands as if she were telling me a funny story.

She whispered to me.

"Gracie, they *are* watching you. Not me, not anyone else in the room. The older man took a photo of us on his phone. They've got a black bag with them, and they keep looking down at it."

I felt the blood drain from my face. Had the foreign agents finally gotten me in a corner where they could finish me off? My options—either blow my cover with Elana by letting her know my WITSEC status or face these two men and whatever they intended to do with me.

Talk to Reggie.

The urgent thought popped into my head. I leaned across the bar and caught the bartender's attention.

"Drake, is Reggie around? I need to talk to him."

"He's upstairs in his office," Drake said as he squirted tonic water into a glass. "He said he'll be down for the next act, though, if you want to—"

"There are some men here that I think could be trouble for me. They're sitting in front of the fireplace. Is there a way to get upstairs to Reggie's office without being seen?"

Drake thought for a moment. He glanced over at the fireplace area. "Why don't I call Reggie and tell him to come down? I'll alert security and have them right here by the bar. Should I call the police?"

I thought of the chief and Brad and decided they would be no match for the two if I was right about who they were.

"No, not right now."

Drake knelt down behind the bar. He was talking quietly and calmly on the phone.

I sighed with relief. Now how to approach this with my friend.

"Elana, this has to do with something in my past. I'm not sure what these guys are here to do, but it's a good idea for us to get out of here fast."

Elana took this surprisingly well as she gathered her purse from the bar top and slipped it over her arm. A look of excitement flashed in her eyes. "Does this have something to do with the dead guy on the highway?"

Great. Elana was already trying to make a connection between me and Overcoat Man. I hoped the federal marshals appreciated how hard I was trying *not* to blow my cover in a difficult situation.

"Your guess is as good as mine," I said, deliberately

vague.

Within five minutes, Reggie McFerrin had entered the room. When he walked in, his brow was furrowed above his sunglasses, but as soon as he approached the bar, he put on a congenial smile. He looked over at the fireplace area. The two men were still there. When Reggie looked over at them, they suddenly seemed to be interested in a menu in front of them. Reggie studied the pair from a distance.

"Elana and Gracie, I'd love to chat with you in my office upstairs. Why don't you come upstairs? I hope you've been enjoying the music tonight."

"It was wonderful," Elana said with exaggerated cheerfulness. I could tell she was nervous and unsure what was going to happen next. Reggie leaned over the bar and whispered something to Drake. I heard the words security and police backup.

We both stood up, and I tried not to look back at the two men. Reggie led us back through the dining area, then we went back through the busy kitchen, where workers were chopping vegetables and sautéing them on the large stove. Reggie opened a door that looked like a pantry and we walked inside, where I saw a narrow stairway.

"Sometimes I need to get upstairs fast," he said with a smile.

Reggie stepped quietly up the wooden stairs, so we followed suit. Soon we were on the second floor of the saloon, in front of the office.

We'd taken a different entrance into Reggie's office, a place I'd seen last summer—when musician April Lewis sat sobbing and telling me her life story in Reggie's big purple executive chair.

"You're safe here, Gracie," Reggie said over the pounding of the music from the band downstairs. "I don't know who those two men are, but I've had some experience with unsavory types, and they tend to have a look. Drake and the security team will keep an eye on them. You and Elana are welcome to stay in the suites up here if you don't feel comfortable going home. The bands tonight are local and won't be needing them."

Immediately I thought of my oblivious father. What if these guys went to my house? If Nate were here, I'd call and ask him if he'd stay with my father, which he'd certainly do. But I didn't have that option.

"I can't leave my father by himself tonight." I took a seat in front of his large antique desk. My heart was still pounding, but I felt better now that I was out of the sight of the men. "But I'd like to wait till the men leave."

"Stay up here as long as you need to." Reggie picked up his cell phone and seemed to be checking a text. "Security will make sure no one gets up here. Make yourself comfortable. There's beer in the minifridge and wine in the rack. Help yourself."

"You'll let us know when it's safe to come out?" Elana looked frightened, a look I wasn't used to seeing on her.

Reggie nodded. "We've called the chief to tell him to be on alert."

While I had my doubts that this situation was something River Grove PD could handle, I started to relax a bit.

After Reggie left, Elana went over to the wine rack and picked out a bottle of red. Without saying a word, she ripped off the foil and turned the corkscrew into the cork. She eased it out with a pop. She poured the red wine into glasses and brought them over to the desk.

"All right, Gracie," she said as she settled back into the chair opposite me, an odd look on her face.

"You need to tell me what the hell is going on."

Chapter Eighteen

Elana leaned back in her chair, her legs crossed. She took a big gulp of wine and watched me, waiting for me to answer.

She looked skeptical. As I suspected, she resented that I hadn't been upfront with her.

"It has to do with my ex." I choked out the words.

"Was your ex—*Steve*—I think you told me his name—" She took another gulp of wine and chugged it down. "—was he in the mafia? Was he involved in some kind of criminal activity? Gracie, you're not telling me anything. I don't know if your life is in danger. Or if mine is. For all I know you're the criminal. And you're hiding out here in River Grove."

"Elana, if I were in trouble with the law, why would I have worked with the chief? He could easily look up my police record."

Actually, he couldn't—at least not for my old name. Grace Hollis Morrison had been erased from all government records. I took a sip of the wine and escaped into a deep, rich well of flavor. Berry jam, an edge of oak, and a finish that settled in like chocolate on my tongue. For a few seconds, I existed only in this very satisfying glass of wine. But I knew that if Elana or anyone else googled me or looked me up on social media—a place I avoided—they would see almost nothing about Gracie Markley. I had no presence on social media and couldn't be tagged on photos people posted. No one could search for me on Instagram, Facebook, Twitter or any similar apps.

I began to explain, as much as I could.

"My ex was involved in criminal activity. When I found out, I spoke up about it. He associated with some dangerous people. Now they're after me."

I felt a sense of relief when I got the words out. I was telling the truth. It felt like a drink of fresh, cold water after a long hike in a desert of lies.

Not sure if LaValle and Piccelli would approve, but I didn't have much choice given the situation. How else was I supposed to explain the appearance of the two men? I was a little surprised that Reggie had done so much for me tonight, without asking for more explanation.

Elana sat back in her chair and sighed as if she were still trying to come to terms with what I'd revealed.

Drums pounded from the music downstairs. The floor shook under my feet.

Elana watched me for a while then shook her head and let out a heavy sigh.

"Oh, God. This really happened to you, didn't it? It all makes sense now. You never talked about your time in the Northwest. I had to pry to get anything out of you. You were afraid I would tell everyone in town your secrets." There was hurt in her eyes. "I wish you could have trusted me."

"You're my best friend. I wanted to." My eyes teared up. "But it's complicated."

Elana swirled her wine glass and looked down into it. "I told you all about my life, my marriage, my problems at work. I don't want a friend who can't do the same with me."

We sat in uneasy silence for a few minutes. I wanted to say something to make things right, to fix things between us. I'd been as honest as I could be without blowing my cover. I didn't feel I could say any more. At WITSEC orientation, a therapist had warned me of the realities of assuming a new identity. It would affect my relationships and my mental health. I was living it now.

I heard footsteps on the stairs we'd used before. Reggie opened the door.

"They're gone," he said calmly. "Drake said they got up and searched the downstairs area, then finally took their bag and cleared out. I'd called the chief and told him about the situation. Brad came over in the squad car. When the men left, he followed them until they turned onto Highway 1, heading north."

I immediately called my father to make sure he was okay. In a groggy voice, he asked if Elana and I were going to stay at the Riverside. He'd spent a quiet evening watching a retrospective on Elizabeth II's reign. I told him I'd be home soon.

"Thank you, Reggie." I got up and hugged him. He smelled like sandalwood and spices.

He walked Elana and I downstairs, where the headlining band was still rocking the place at a very high decibel level. After wishing us well, Reggie stood at the side of the stage, engaged in what he loved: people playing and enjoying music.

Elana drove me home in silence. As she pulled up in

front of the carport, she rubbed her eyes and looked over at me.

"Well, Gracie. It's certainly been an interesting evening," she said coldly. "I hope this situation works out for you. I wish you luck. Goodbye."

I didn't know if that meant goodbye forever or goodbye, like, *when this blows over, let's get together and have a glass of wine.*

She watched me as I shut the car door, then she quickly backed out of our driveway.

I unlocked the front door, tears stinging my eyes. What could I have done differently? I couldn't tell her about Ben and his friend Kyle's arrest and my testimony at the trial. Or how painful it was to realize Ben was not the man I thought I'd married.

There was no way I could share with her on the same level she did with me.

This hurt almost more than if I'd broken up with Nate.

Biga came in and snuggled next to me.

He was scruffy, obsessed with food, and fickle in his affections.

But he was my built-in friend and, like most dogs, loved unconditionally.

Which is what I needed tonight.

Chapter Nineteen

The next morning I was wide awake and ready to get up at 3:30 a.m.

The problem was, it was Saturday.

The Laughing Loaf opened at 8 today, and I didn't have to be at the bakery till 5:30 a.m.

During the night, Biga had tucked his warm little body under my arm. When I looked down, I saw his nose poking straight into my armpit. I laughed, despite everything that had happened last night.

I felt for my phone on the nightstand and saw that Nate had texted.

Bet you had fun last night with Elana. No hangover this morning?

I tapped on my phone, not even wanting to address what happened last night at The Riverside.

No hangover!

It hurt when I thought about Elana's comments last night.

But at least she, Reggie, Drake, and Brad Castro had taken my fears seriously. Their coordinated efforts kept the two men from getting to me.

Though there was no guarantee they wouldn't come back.

Extra cautious this morning, I brought two things with me to the bakery: my little watchdog, and a heavy camping flashlight that Nate had brought over when he'd been teaching my dad to barbecue in the backyard on summer nights. I figured it would help me see any threat on my way in to the bakery. It would also do some damage if I were to hit an intruder with it.

Biga didn't want to get into his crate, so I threw a treat in. Of course, he went right in, and I quickly latched the crate, feeling like an evil supervillain or the town dog catcher.

Once we got in the back door of The Laughing Loaf, I locked it and turned on every light in the place. Afraid that I wouldn't hear an intruder if the music was my usual listening fare, I put on a playlist of quiet acoustic pop. It wasn't as energizing, but it calmed me.

Beck came in with her wicker egg basket and gave me a funny look.

"What is this music?" She asked once she'd put the eggs away and greeted Biga. "Did you have a hard night last night? Should I keep my voice down?" She giggled.

"Very funny. I didn't party that hard last night," I smiled as I rolled out the cinnamon roll dough. "I just felt like listening to more relaxing music this morning."

"Right, Gracie," Beck said with a skeptical look on her face. She went over to the industrial fridge to pull out the beignet dough for cutting. "I mean, it's nice music. I'm just used to the jumping '80s music. It's so energizing."

"Maybe when we close today," I said, as I shaped whole wheat walnut biga loaves on the metal table. Shaping loaves was a kind of a contemplative ritual for me. I pressed down and turned the loaves on the metal surface, till the force and friction tightened them and made them more compact. I soon had a table full of identical, tight, round boules, which would be ready to bake later this morning.

As I turned the round loaves, I felt relief that we wouldn't be inundated by high schoolers this morning, though there were always some who stopped by for coffee on the weekends. It would be a quiet, relatively relaxed Saturday at the bakery. Customers would come in and linger over coffee and baked goods in the dining area. Parents would drink coffee and talk while their children drew or played games at the tables.

Maybe I'd been thinking of the high schoolers in the wrong way--as badly behaved customers who needed to be served then herded out quickly before the adults came in.

I wondered if the students might actually be helpful as I looked into the murder of Overcoat Man. I still wanted to know who he was and why he'd come here.

Before we opened, I set the joke of the day on its rack on the counter.

Laughing Loaf Joke of the Day
Why did the hipster burn his mouth?
Because he ate his pizza before it was cool.

Around 9 a.m., a few high schoolers came in who were on their way to RGHS to do setup for next week's home-coming festivities. There were activities every day leading up to the big football game on the following Friday. One of the young women who came in was up for homecoming queen. Jeb Walker, one of the seniors who spilled his coffee that day of the murder, was nominated for homecoming king. I hadn't been involved in any homecoming-related activities in high school, so I was genuinely curious as to how they worked.

"How does this homecoming queen and king thing work exactly?" I asked Emma Dooley, a junior, who was involved in student government at RGHS. After she ordered, I threw in a joke. "If a king and queen win, are they obligated by law to date each other?"

Emma and the friend behind her, Carly, started laughing.

"Okay, first of all—*no*," Emma said, once she'd stopped laughing. "The student body votes, then whatever guy and girl gets the most votes get to be king and queen. The runners-up still dress up and come out on the field at half-time at the game. Sometimes people are nominated as a joke. Just because it's funny. Skyler Robbins was nominated by a lot of people this year and he might even win. He's so hilarious."

Skyler. That must be Sky, the other lanky young man who "helped" spill the coffee. There'd been some competitiveness between him and Jeb that day.

"Thanks for filling me in, Emma." I handed Emma her latte, along with a plate with two cinnamon rolls.

A few students later, Sky came to the front of the line, looking sheepish. He was wearing a t-shirt that read: *Why be part of the problem when you can be the whole problem?*

"Hey, Gracie. I'll have French Toast sticks and a dark chocolate mocha. Make sure Beck puts lots of whipped cream on it."

Beck looked back from the espresso machine and laughed. "Only if you ask me nicely."

I pulled out a box of French Toast sticks and set it down on the counter for him.

"I hear you have a pretty good chance of winning homecoming king this year."

He shrugged and blinked at me. "Yeah. Well, my friends nominated me. So what can you do?"

Sky was pretty social. I had a feeling he'd be a good person to ask.

"Question for you, Sky. Did you notice a new kid around town—maybe last week? He may have been hanging out with kids downtown. Tall and skinny, blond hair."

Sky thought about this and nodded. "Yeah, a bunch of us saw a dude who looked like that at RG's. Blond hair and wearing a coat. But he didn't go to River Grove. He said he was visiting someone in town."

Could this have been Overcoat Man? He looked like he belonged with these students. He looked close to their age. If this was Overcoat Man, it was an interesting comment on how oblivious teenagers were to the news adults watched and listened to. They had their own channels for news and communication. They hadn't heard the sheriff's and the chief's calls for help in identifying the murdered man. At the least, they hadn't connected the kid they'd met at the pizza parlor with news of the man killed on the highway.

"Did he say who he was visiting?"

Sky shook his head and opened his box of French toast sticks. He started dipping them in syrup and popping them into his mouth.

"Did he say where he was from, by any chance?"

Sky shook his head. "Naw. Don't think so."

After his mocha arrived on the counter topped with a

large mound of whipped cream, Sky blew an exaggerated kiss to Beck and me on his way out the door.

When I went into the back room to put the whole wheat loaves in the oven, I thought about what to do. I had enough information to go to the chief. He could start questioning the students who had seen the kid downtown. He'd probably be happy to receive some break in the case. I thought of the students I'd seen hang out with Sky. Jeb, for sure, and maybe any seniors who might drop by for coffee on a Saturday morning.

I brought out the second big tray of cinnamon rolls, which had been cooling, and restocked the display case. Then I went to tidy the cabinet with the napkins, straws, cup sleeves and sugar and cinnamon shakers, right by the big table. Jeb had just come in and was sitting at a table by himself, blinking at a diagram in a textbook, which looked like physics to me.

"Hey, Jeb. How's it going?"

He just groaned, then turned to me sadly. "AP Physics is the worst."

"My dad's a retired physics professor." I said as I refilled a napkin dispenser. "It's definitely not my thing, but if you ever need help with it, he loves to tutor students." Not sure I should speak for my dad, but I was pretty sure he'd be excited to help someone struggling with the concepts.

Jeb lifted his head with interest. "I'd be up for that. The stuff makes my head hurt."

"Mine, too." I widened my eyes and nodded. "Hey, this is a random question. Did you by any chance see a kid hanging out downtown last week, maybe by RG's? Tall, blond and skinny."

He sat back in his chair, stretching his legs out under the table, and let out a sigh. "Umm, maybe. There was a guy

I hadn't seen before, when Sky and some of us were getting pizza last week."

"Did he say what his name was?" I tried to sound casual. "Or where he was from?"

He yawned, which made me think he'd probably stayed up late last night studying.

"Don't remember any name. But he talked about being from up north. I think—Seattle? That's what he said."

It was one of those moments where time stops abruptly. Where two things mash together in a completely unexpected coincidence. My two lives intersected for a moment, and I felt a sudden jolt.

"Thanks, Jeb. I wondered if it was someone I knew. Guess not."

And that was a complete lie.

Chapter Twenty

This easy, laidback Saturday morning could not go by fast enough for me.

Focusing on the bakes, I pulled trays of whole wheat walnut raisin biga loaves out of the oven, then slid in the batch of brioche loaves. In between, while some sourdough loaves proofed, I baked scones and another large tray of cinnamon rolls.

I wasn't being my usual friendly self to customers, but I managed to serve everyone, trading places with Beck to fill in on the espresso machine when she needed to fry up another batch of beignets.

When things quieted down, I scrolled through Twitter and found Kayden's profile on Twitter.

I enlarged it and snapped a screen shot.

Please customers, order and leave. I need to get over to city hall to talk to the chief.

I got my chance at 10:30 a.m. Beck would cover everything while I dashed across the street.

Peony Roberts wasn't manning the City Hall front desk on Saturdays, so I made my way down the hall without hindrance. When I passed her office, Mayor C stood up and moved to her doorway, calling out to me.

"Hey, Gracie—can I talk to you for a minute?"

"After I talk to the chief!" I shouted as I passed her startled face.

I tapped on the chief's open door. He sat slumped over his coffee, in front of a plate with a half-eaten beignet on it. Judging by the circles under his eyes, he hadn't slept much.

"Glad to see you're okay, after those two men threatened you at the Riverside," he said wearily.

Last night's scary events felt like days ago to me. I was a woman on a mission.

"Dave, I have information about the man killed on the highway."

His mouth fell open. He stood up and pulled the uncomfortable captain's chair around to the front of his desk for me. Then he closed the door.

"I thought I'd ask some of the high schoolers if they happened to see an unfamiliar person in town, someone around their age." I had to be careful with what I said. I was pretty sure the chief knew more about my situation than he'd let on. But if I told him too much, I could mess things up. As a law enforcement professional, he was held to a certain level of confidentiality—but he was also the head of the police force in a very small town. A town where gossip spread faster than local wildfires during dry season. Things the chief had told other people had already made the rounds in River Grove, like when he'd told Cheryl at Cut and Curl that he thought Overcoat Man was Russian.

I took a deep breath.

"The pictures of the man on the highway made him look so young. I wondered if it was possible these kids had run into him, maybe at RGs."

For the first time in days, the chief looked alert, hopeful even. He leaned forward over his desk.

"What did they say?"

"They did see him at RG's. They talked to him at least a little. He said he was from Seattle." I swallowed hard. This kid was someone I'd known.

When I thought about the photo of the body the chief showed me, I tried hard to reconcile it with the kid I once knew. A dead body doesn't have the mannerisms and expressions of the living person inhabiting it.

Kayden had come over to our house to play video games with his older brother Kyle Burnett and my ex-husband Ben. He'd been barely sixteen at the time, a skinny kid who followed his older brother around and idolized him. I'd seen him in court, heartbroken and angry that his role model had been arrested. He sneered at me during my testimony and even told a reporter that I was a liar and had made up the story of Ben and Kyle selling secrets.

Had he come to River Grove to avenge his brother by retaliating against the person who turned him in?

I had to fudge the next part.

"I looked him up online, based on some details the kids told me. I found a photo on social media and it's him. His name was Kayden. Kayden Burnett. As far as I know, he was eighteen, not much older than the River Grove HS seniors he was hanging out with."

A wave of exhaustion came over me after getting all this information out. "By the way, the high schoolers knew someone had been killed on the highway. But they hadn't seen the news stories asking for help in identifying the body on the highway. They didn't make the connection."

I hoped the chief would contact Kayden's family in

Seattle, so they could know what had happened to their missing son.

I also hoped the chief would not ask me how I knew all this.

The chief scribbled notes on his yellow legal tablet.

Then he stopped and looked at me directly.

"I'll have to verify this. Thank you for this information, Gracie." He studied my face thoughtfully. "Do you think it would be helpful to talk to the teenagers any further?"

Sky and Jeb would tell the chief they hadn't known the kid's name. I'd filled in that part.

"It sounded like they didn't get to know much about him other than what I told you, chief. They'd just chatted with him at the pizza parlor."

I took out my phone and showed him the screen shot I'd snapped from Twitter.

The chief put on his reading glasses and peered at it.

"Okay. There is a resemblance," he said after I pulled the phone away. He gobbled down the last of his beignet and turned to his desk phone. He looked like a relieved man, now that he could tell the county sheriff that River Grove no longer needed their help. "If you'll excuse me, Gracie, I've got some calls to make."

I headed down the hall, preparing to go back to The Laughing Loaf, when I was pulled in by Mayor C. Quite literally. She grabbed my arm and pulled me into her office.

"Hold on a minute, Gracie."

"What's going on with you?" She demanded, her eyes narrowing. "I heard there were some men stalking you last night at The Riverside. Everyone's talking about it today. Thank God, Brad Castro chased them out of town."

I nodded and leaned against the doorframe wearily.

"I hope they don't come back," I said weakly, pretty sure

that the two men would return after their unsuccessful mission. "Reggie kept Elana and I up in his office until it was safe to come out."

"Reggie seems very protective of you." The mayor gave me an assessing look. "I guess if you were being stalked, the best place for you was The Riverside."

I wondered what her comment meant. Could Reggie McFerrin be the local contact keeping watch over us? A ridiculous thought, that this aging former hippie, who dressed in purple and black and never took off his sunglasses, would be a federal agent. Still, in the past year and a half, I found out that Reggie was a man of surprises.

"Corinne, I've got to get back to the bakery."

"Be careful, Gracie." The mayor prepared to get back to work. "Don't go off on your own. No more walks along the river with your dog. That little pipsqueak isn't going to save you."

I headed across the street to the bakery, feeling worse than I had when I rushed over to the chief. Kayden Burnett, somebody who had hung out at my house in Seattle, was dead. And the two men stalking me were out there somewhere.

And, as much as I loved my little dog, Mayor C had a point.

Chapter Twenty-One

When I returned home for the day, I told my father everything that had happened at The Riverside the night before, and Elana's reaction to the secrets I'd kept from her. And Jeb and Sky's identification of Kayden Burnett. It was a relief to get everything out.

"For every action, there's an equal and opposite reaction." He patted my arm at the table, as we enjoyed cups of tea with some cranberry orange scones I'd brought home. "I'm sorry you had to bear the consequences of speaking up, my dear. You did the right thing. Kayden and the Burnett family gave you a lot of grief in court. It's certainly possible that he came down here to retaliate against you for turning in his brother."

"He was so young. And shorter then, too. A nerdy and clueless kid. I remember him playing video games in my kitchen, chowing down the bread I'd made. He even told me, 'Grace, your bread is so good, you should start a bakery.' Dang, I was so *nice* to him, too." Biga jumped up onto my lap and rubbed his head on my arm. "If he was out to get me, who killed him?"

"But what if Kayden wasn't out to get you?" My father got that look in his eye, the kind he got when he was testing out an idea. He sat back in his seat and tapped his chin as he thought.

I tried to stifle a yawn. "What do you mean?"

"Maybe Kayden had a change of heart. Maybe he came down from Seattle to warn you someone was coming after you."

Remembering Kayden's behavior back during the trials, this couldn't possibly be true. I snorted at him.

"Dad, what happened to Ockham's Razor—the simplest explanation is the most likely to be true? The last I saw of Kayden, he was really mad at me. He thought I made up lies about Kyle selling secrets. If he wanted to help me, it would be a huge turnaround."

My father picked up his last piece of scone and ate it.

"Children grow up. Sometimes they realize their idols weren't who they thought they were."

What he was saying seemed unlikely. For this to be true, Kayden would have to have figured out that the two men knew where I lived and were coming after me.

I thought of the night I'd come back from taking Nate to the airport. Overcoat Man—who I now knew was Kayden— had come up to our front porch.

Maybe he wasn't there to kill us or confront me. What if he'd been there to warn me that the foreign agents were coming?

I'd screamed at him and chased him away.

* * *

After dinner, I went to my room and opened my laptop.

Other than my lucky guess about Twitter, I had no idea what social media Kayden Burnett had been on. Not Facebook; that would be an older crowd. Instagram didn't seem like a place he'd hang out. If I was lucky, he'd had some kind of a blog or microblog.

I googled his name.

I did find an Instagram account with the name Kayden Burnett, but it was run by a twenty-something fashion influencer, and it featured photographs of a heavily made-up young woman modeling clothes and shoes.

I went back to Twitter. The sour look on his face and sharp features seemed to match the kid I remembered. The few posts were short blurbs about video games. And some reviews of games, if a review could be as simple as "[Insert name of game]: This game sucks."

I looked for any cross posting of a blog but couldn't find any among his posts.

On an online forum for video games, I found some posts from Kayden Burnett, with the same photo from Twitter, dated over the past year.

One featured an animated GIF of a monster holding a skyscraper in his hand, in the process of smashing a city.

Ever been destroyed by someone? Someone you looked up to? I was completely fooled by him and his friend. Now I know the truth of what he did. He lied to us all.

The post attracted concerned replies from friends:

Kayd, you okay?

So sorry to hear about your bro. Stay safe!
If you want to talk, call me, Kayden!
OMG. That bites, K. Love you!

My dad might have been right. Kayden realized after his brother's trial and sentencing there was proof that Kyle and Ben had sold tech secrets. His brother had let him down.

I groaned. *Welcome to the club, Kayden.*

I searched the rest of the posts. They were up and down. In many of them, Kayden vented his anger against his brother. In others, he vowed that he would be nothing like his brother, and that he had a new plan for his life, to do better. To be as different from Kyle as he could.

The most recent post featured a photo of a superhero zooming down from the sky, with flaming fists.

One of the worst things I ever did was to treat an honest person badly. She tried to do the right thing, but she got trashed just like me. I think she's in trouble. Kyle says she's got something, and I don't think she knows it. I need to find her.

How had he found me? I thought of the bread. Kayden had loved the bread I made. I wonder if he'd looked up bakeries and searched till he found a place that made the kind of baked goods he remembered eating in my kitchen: brioche, whole wheat raisin walnut biga. Cinnamon rolls with my secret caramel sauce. He could have found that on The Laughing Loaf's website.

Now I remembered the photo he had in his pocket. It must have been taken in our backyard in Seattle, when we were having a picnic lunch with Ben and his friends. Kayden must have taken it himself.

My throat choked with emotion. Kayden had come down to California because he'd known there were people coming to get me. But that part – "She's got something and I don't think she knows it."

What did I *have*?

It was 8:30 p.m. I should call and tell the agents.

Nate, who was as predictable as clockwork, would text at 9 p.m.

I used my dad's burner phone to make the call. Per usual, he'd left it sitting in plain sight on his office desk.

"Gracie. Glad you called," LaValle answered, sounding stressed. "You beat me to it. We know about the men tracking you, and we know who they are. You're in serious danger, Gracie. We're working on your relocation right now. Piccelli and I will be at your house tomorrow at 6 p.m. Plans are to move you and your father out of River Grove tomorrow night."

Chapter Twenty-Two

I felt sick to my stomach.

"What?"

"That's no warning at all. I have a business to run. I can't leave now."

I absolutely couldn't. I thought of Beck, who loved her job and had been preparing to take classes and grow in her craft at The Laughing Loaf. And all the noisy teenagers who started their day at the bakery. And Mayor C and the chief holding their public safety meetings at the corner table.

And Nate.

"Gracie, these men are Russian agents. Trained killers for the Kremlin. This assignment came from the top. We didn't realize they were in the country until they showed up at The Riverside."

I told him the results of my recent research.

"Jeremy, the man shot on the highway was Kayden Burnett, Kyle Burnett's little brother. The chief verified this and talked to his family in Seattle. I read Kayden's posts on a video game forum tonight. He came down here to warn me that two men were after me."

"Who would have thought the kid would change sides?" Jeremy said softly. "And he was killed because of it. That's all the more reason why you and your father need to relocate as soon as possible. Your lives are in danger, Gracie. Trust us with this. You and your father need to get out immediately. These men will be back. They're not going to be scared off by some deputy chasing them away."

What did the men want? I wondered if I'd inadvertently brought something down to California with me, something the Russians wanted. Could Ben have stashed secret papers or files in something I'd brought with me? I thought about everything I'd brought with me that Ben may have had access to.

"Jeremy, what can I do—if it's something I don't even *know* that I have?" I rubbed my eyes. My body needed sleep, but thoughts were whizzing around my head at high speed. "Maybe there was one last transfer of classified information Ben wanted to make that day, before he was arrested. But if that's true, I have no idea what it was. Or where it could be."

"Piccelli and I are on it. We'll go over the original documents recovered from Ben's computer in Seattle. We'll do that tonight. We might get some clues as to what it is."

"Tell me," I said in a hoarse voice. "Where will we be relocated?"

"Right now it looks like Alabama," LaValle said matter-of-factly. "But we'll give you a more specific location tomorrow. A truck will come tomorrow night at 10 p.m. with movers who'll get you packed up and begin the transfer of your belongings. It works best to do this at night."

Alabama?

I'd never even been to the Southern United States. I couldn't imagine being happy there. Or anywhere other than River Grove.

I went into the living room to tell my dad about the relocation. He took it without much reaction, like he tended to take bad news; he thanked me for telling him, then he began watching a video lecture on quantum physics on his iPad.

We both had our escapes. I baked. He got lost in the world of theories and equations.

At 9 p.m., I got Nate's text.

> 2 days! Ready to be done with this place.
> Can't wait to see you. Wanna talk?

My throat was so constricted, I wasn't sure I could get words out. This would be the last time I talked to Nate. I considered ghosting him again. Maybe it would be easier for us to end things now. Though nothing would make this easy.

Should I follow Reggie's advice and enjoy the short time we had left? I could hear Nate's voice one last time. I considered telling him the truth about everything tonight. I wanted so badly to be honest with him. Who I really was and what I'd been through in Seattle. Who Overcoat Man was and why we were leaving.

I wanted to be myself with Nate. He deserved that.

I texted back that I could talk.

I let my phone ring twice, and then I picked up, my heart pounding. It would have been easier to ignore it. I tried to work up a cheerful tone.

"Hey, how is my favorite bird nerd?"

"I guess that fits me." Nate laughed with that rumble in his chest. "I'm tired of climbing over rocks. I got some great shots this week. No more cliff dives, either."

"Please tell me you stopped risking it all for that one perfect shot."

He chuckled. "I've actually risked my life a few times this week."

"Do you have a bird picture you could send me, now?" I wanted to hear the delight in his voice as he described the bird to me. Capture that joy and tuck it away forever.

"Sure, I'll send you one now. I was going to email you a whole portfolio. Some beautiful shots."

Soon a photo appeared in the text thread. A little grey bird with a small-pointed beak. He looked toward the camera with big round eyes, tilting his head slightly, as if he were asking a question. He looked adorable and almost animated, as if he were one of the birds that fluttered around Snow White as she cleaned house.

"This guy's a warbler finch. He's a small one. He goes for the insects and grubs after the rains, getting the good stuff, while the larger beaked birds fight over the scarce seeds and nuts. He is—what did you say before? Plucky. Maybe even *scrappy*."

"I like him a lot."

"Have you thought about a getaway when I get back?"

My throat tightened even more. "Nate, it's been a hard week. I haven't even gotten a chance to think about it."

He was quiet for a while.

"Sorry to push, Gracie. Take your time."

Suddenly words came to me, and I blurted them out.

"I want you to know, Nate. I really care for you. If anything happens to me, remember that."

"Gracie, what are you saying?" His voice sounded hoarse, full of worry. "What's going on? Talk to me."

"Nate, I have to go." I pressed to end the call.

I silenced my phone so I couldn't hear anything more from him then shut my eyes tight.

Biga jumped up on the bed and settled in next to me.

I heard my dad come in and call my name. I opened one eye and saw him silhouetted in the doorway.

He waited for a while.

When he didn't get a response, he turned off the lights and quietly shut my door.

Chapter Twenty-Three

Today would be my last day at the bakery.

I got up at 3:30, unable to sleep. I showered, dressed, and found a clean apron.

When I went back into my room, my little dog was still asleep.

"Biga. You going with me?"

He lifted his head, looked at me for a while, then dove back into the covers.

"So that's a *no* then."

I'd have lots of time to bond with him once we got to Alabama or wherever we ended up. I would sit and cuddle with him, while trying to figure out what the heck had happened to my life and whether I'd ever be free from the consequences of turning in my tech spy husband and his friend.

It's a very strange experience to go through the routines of a day, the mundane things you normally do without thinking, knowing this is the last time you'll do them. Each thing seems significant. And I thought at the time, if I thoughtfully and carefully did each one in my day, I could actually slow down time. I could make this day last.

I turned on all the lights in the bakery then put on my usual, fun 80s music mix, which Beck would appreciate. I checked the proofer, which had done its job perfectly. I threw myself into shaping brioche dough into loaves and mixing the final ingredients into the whole wheat raisin walnut dough for its bulk rise. I closed my eyes and inhaled the sweet yeasty aromas. I felt the soft warm dough in my hands.

I mixed up another batch of cranberry and orange scones, just in case.

Then I went to fill a bag with things from my office that I'd take with me. Running shorts and a jacket I'd never actually run the trail in, as I'd intended. And a few treat bags and some dog toys I rarely used with Biga. One was a treat ball you were supposed to fill with treats, which were dispensed as your pet played with it. Biga could never figure out how to get the treats out and usually gave up.

When Beck came in, carrying the basket with eggs from her chickens, she started singing along loudly to Duran Duran's "Rio."

"Caramel apple tarts, ready to go for this morning," she said cheerfully, pulling out a tray with the beautiful baked tarts. "I tried to ramp up a little with the demand like you said, Gracie. I thought three dozen was about right, thinking of how many people weren't able to get them yesterday."

"That sounds right on, Beck. I think the strategy's working."

This morning I offered to cut and fry the beignets so Beck could work on French toast sticks. I was trying to come to terms with the fact that as of tomorrow, The Laughing Loaf would be no more. As I slipped beignets into the hot oil, I reminded myself to print Beck a substantial severance check before leaving and put it out for her to find in the morning.

I set out the joke of the day. For my last day, it seemed timely, and maybe a little passive aggressive.

Laughing Loaf Joke of the Day
Why don't people like Russian dolls?
Because they're full of themselves.

When we opened at 8 a.m., a few couples came by with their dogs, got their coffee, and went to sit at the outside tables.

Sky and Jeb came in at 8:30. Sky wore a paper crown from Burger King. He'd already claimed the title of home-coming king for himself.

"Nice crown, Sky." I handed him his French toast sticks and latte.

"Trying to prepare in advance for my role," he said with a straight face.

"Dress for the job you want." I smiled.

Sky nodded and barely caught his crown as it started to roll off.

Right behind Sky's back, Jeb rolled his eyes. "Real mature, Sky. That'll be a chai latte for me, Gracie. And French toast sticks, of course." He leaned toward me and lowered his voice. "Hey, were you serious when you said your dad could tutor me in AP Physics?"

"I can tell him you're interested." Which I could, even though it would never happen.

"Awesome, Gracie."

The chief came in at 9 and got in line. When his turn came to order, I noticed his eyes were puffy.

He leaned in toward me, almost whispering. "How are you holding up?"

"Okay," I said tentatively. When I looked at his face I could tell. "You know we're leaving tonight."

He nodded and looked around. "I'm so sorry."

"Does Mayor C know?"

The chief shook his head. Another person ticked off the list. Mayor C wasn't the local contact.

"These men want something I have," I said quietly. "Something my ex-husband stashed in my stuff. I have no idea what it is. The agents think they're coming back."

"This town won't be the same without you," he swallowed, his eyes watering. He sighed. "Damn it, Gracie, if I'm ordering my last beignets, give me six. And a Cherry Orchard Latte."

After he finished paying, I whispered *thank you*. It made me feel better that he knew what I was going through, on a day no one else was able to acknowledge it.

Annie Morton came in to pick up coffee and cinnamon rolls for Eric, who was waiting outside with Pixie. I wanted to hug these people, say goodbye to my friends, like any normal person would when they were going away. But I couldn't. Instead, I smiled and handed her two lattes and a clamshell of rolls. I darted into the back room and dug down in my bag to grab a treat from my stash of dog goodies for Pixie. And told Annie to have a good day.

Jake Daniels came by to pick up a half dozen of the tarts to take to Aiden and his mom. Then Cheryl from Cut and Curl and her husband ordered tarts and hung out with their drinks in the dining area for a while. Peter James Jordan, attorney at law, came in after church with his elderly mother, Marjorie. Apparently, he was introducing her to the joys of drinking lat-*tays*.

A few people came into the bakery from Santa Cruz. They'd read the article in the *Sentinel*.

All in all, a pretty normal day.

I hadn't seen or heard from Elana since that night at the Riverside. And I hadn't even checked my phone to see if Nate had responded any further to our conversation last night. Reggie hadn't made an appearance at The Laughing Loaf in a few days. Three people who'd meant so much to me during my time in River Grove.

But by the time I locked the front door at 2 p.m. at the end of our business day, I was emotionally exhausted.

Beck put on another 80s mix. She was singing along to the Katrina and the Waves song, "Walking on Sunshine," even dancing around the back room in between mixing tart crust and chopping up kale and herbs.

"Gracie!" She called out between lyrics. "I registered for that class at the Baking Institute. The one on eclairs and profiteroles. I'm super excited. Last night I tried playing around with choux pastry at home."

"You're going to be great at it," I smiled. "You're feeling okay going up to the city by yourself?" I almost wanted to give her a lesson or two on navigating a city, what areas to avoid and how not to walk around looking like an easy mark for cons. But like everything else I wanted to do in my last day here, there was no time, and it wasn't going to happen.

"I'll be fine, Gracie." She fit crust into a tart pan. "I know I have to leave River Grove some time in order to improve my baking skills. There are things I can't do here. Taking professional classes is one of them."

Beck was ten years younger than me, but she was the

closest thing I had to a child or a sibling. And she was growing up.

"Beck, I'll close up today. I've got some spreadsheets to work on." I tried to keep from crying. "When you finish up the tarts, why don't you work on your choux pastry at home?"

When she'd finished up and put the tarts on the cooling racks, she gathered her things together, grabbed her wicker basket and turned to leave.

I went over and hugged her.

"You're amazing, Beck. Just wanted you to know that."

"Aww, Gracie. I already know that."

Beck grinned and practically danced out to her car in the back alley, probably dreaming of choux pastry creations.

I sat for a while in my office. Everything felt surreal right now.

I printed out a generous severance check for Beck, then slipped it into an envelope and wrote her name on it with a simple note.

Even if you stay here, I know you'll go far.
Love, G

* * *

By the time I finished packing up, it was 3:30 p.m.

LaValle and Piccelli would meet us in two and a half hours. I needed to pack, but I was having a hard time making myself walk out the door of The Laughing Loaf.

I broke down Biga's pen and set the panels by the back door. I found a large bin in the store room for hauling them out to my car. After unlocking the compartment behind my desk, I slipped the burner phone into my jacket pocket.

I thought about it for a moment and decided to leave my computer, though I deleted my emails and a folder of personal files.

Then I set down all the bags I needed to take out to my car.

When I dropped the bag with dog toys and treats, I heard a strange rattle. It didn't sound like any dog toy Biga had. It didn't sound like dog treats either. Probably because I was delaying leaving the bakery, I plunged my hands into the bag to investigate.

I pulled out several bags of treats. And three squeaky dog toys, a leash, a harness and a small plastic ball, that looked a little like the Star Wars Death Star, but made out of lime green plastic. Biga's treat dispensing ball.

I shook it and heard the rattle. It was something hard. Plastic or metal.

I put my fingers into the hole and fished around inside. It took me a while to chase the thing around with my fingers, but I managed to grasp it between two fingers and pull it out.

It was a bright red thumb drive, for storing computer files.

Chapter Twenty-Four

After locking the back door, I ran to my car, my heart pounding.

Crunching down the gravelly alley, I drove home at a speed, which—including short cuts—probably broke every River Grove traffic ordinance.

I unlocked the front door and barreled into the house, almost trampling Biga, who'd apparently been by the door, awaiting my return.

My father was sitting in his office at his computer, reading a paper.

"Dad, I need to use your computer. I need to see what this is." I gave him a disapproving look. "Also, you're supposed to be getting ready, not reading articles on thermodynamics."

With a guilty look on his face, my dad slid his rolling office chair back. I moved in and plugged the thumb drive into the USB port.

Then I clicked on the thumb drive's icon on the desktop screen.

There were several numbered image files.

I clicked on an image, and slowly a detailed diagram began to fill the screen. A blueprint of a sleek, streamlined plane, long and very flat. It was unlike anything I'd seen before. It looked almost like an alien spaceship.

I clicked on the next numbered image file. It was a breakout drawing, a close-up on the alien plane, labeled WEAPONS BAY. A box to the side showed a bomb in place, ready to be launched from the plane.

Chills ran over my skin. I knew very little about military aircraft, but this looked like a pretty advanced military bomber plane. My father, staring at the diagram, turned pale.

"This has to be what the Russians are looking for." I turned to my dad. "We've found it."

My father moved closer to peer at the image. "Where was it?"

"In Biga's treat ball."

I had no idea why Ben would have put the thumb drive in Biga's treat ball, but he did. Knowing he'd be arrested soon, maybe he panicked, not wanting to be found with it.

I remembered the day after his arrest, I came back to the house to collect the rest of my and Biga's things and shoved it all in bags. We'd had it all along.

Now that I thought of it, I did have the prickly feeling that someone had been in our house. Here and there around the house, things weren't where I'd left them. Books seemed to have shifted on our shelves. My computer desk wasn't organized the way I'd left it. The FBI had come to collect Ben's computer and devices, but I wouldn't have been surprised if the Russians had also come through looking for the files Ben had promised them.

I pulled the burner phone from my jacket pocket and called the agents.

"I found it. This is what they're looking for. A schematic for a very high-tech plane."

Piccelli answered tersely. "That's what we suspected. We have a meeting now at the federal building in San Francisco. We'll be there in an hour."

My dad handed me the thumb drive and reluctantly closed down his computer and went back to his bedroom. I could hear the scraping noise as he pulled his suitcase down off the closet shelf.

In a daze, I went to my room and took clothes out of my dresser to pack. My body moved in slow motion. I didn't want to be doing this. I had to shut down all thoughts in order to keep moving: the memory of Nate's rumbling laugh, Elana's crazy dancing at The Riverside, even my growing friendship with Mayor C, and the chief's unexpected sympathy this morning.

I continued throwing clothes out of my drawers and onto the bed, then went to get laundry from the dryer to pack up. Biga lay on the bed giving me funny looks. He'd been through this before in Seattle. Dogs remember things.

I was just about to zip up my suitcase when I heard a loud slam from the front of the house. The door thrown open and a doorknob smacking hard against the wall. It reverberated through the house. Then there were loud footsteps. Boots tromped through our living room and kitchen.

I quickly hid the thumb drive.

"Grace Morrison. Jonathan Hollis." Loud, heavily accented voices called out our former names. "You have something we were promised. And we have waited long enough."

The men, the same ones I saw at the Riverside, were in our hallways and I could see them now. They carried what looked like military assault weapons, hanging from straps around their chests.

The younger one with the Giants baseball cap and a soul patch poked the nose of his weapon into my bedroom doorway. The older man with greying hair was behind him. Two assault rifles aimed directly at me. I hadn't grown up around guns and these were terrifying.

"Grace. Hand me the thumb drive. We know you have it." He saw the burner phone sticking out of my pocket. "And give me that phone."

I handed him the burner phone and raised my hands over my head.

"I don't know what you're talking about." My voice held steady. I worried about my father in his office. I was the front guard here and I worried my father was the weakest link. I needed to stop these guys before they got to him.

"Your husband told us. He'd prepared everything for us before he was taken away. Give us the files or prepare to die."

With a sick feeling in my stomach, I stood up slowly, my hands still raised.

"Go ahead and search our house. I can't even imagine what this thing is. I had nothing to do with my husband's work."

The younger man in the ball cap sneered and poked his weapon at me.

"You two killed Kayden, didn't you? Kayden Burnett. He was just a kid. He was only eighteen. You shot him and dropped him off on the side of the road."

"Ah, yes. His brother did very good things for us." he let out a snort. "But Kayden? He insisted on coming to California because he decided he hated what his brother had done. He tried to keep us away from you. He gave us false information on where you were, but we found you anyway when we followed him to your house. He made himself very easy to follow. Very easy to kill. We shot him on the trail then dumped him. What a fool."

"You are asking too many questions, Mrs. Morrison." The ball cap guy whispered to me, shaking his head, and keeping his weapon trained on me. "You don't want to make Dmitri angry. He has a bad temper."

Dmitri, as I now knew his name, stalked down the hall to find my father, and I cringed.

Nestled on my bed, Biga glared up at the man in the ball cap and let out a low growl. I prayed he would stop; these men were unpredictable, on the edge. Who knew when they'd lash out.

The older guy brought my father into my room and, pushing his rifle to the side, tied his hands together with a zip tie. He pushed him down onto the bed near Biga. My dad looked pale, but otherwise calm.

The grey-haired man spoke Russian in a low voice. He seemed to be calling the young guy Serge.

Serge nudged me, keeping the assault rifle pointed at my chest.

Dmitri rooted through my desk drawers. He threw out papers, packets of receipts, and my journals. He unzipped a pencil case and emptied the contents on the floor, then spit out what sounded like curse words in Russian. Finally, he took out all the drawers and dumped them out on the floor. He let out a triumphant cry.

"Serge!"

The young guy kept the rifle pointed at me but looked past me at what the older man was holding. It was a thumb drive. Serge's eyes lit up with excitement.

"Computer!" the older guy barked at him. Serge jerked

his head toward the hall, where a black leather bag sat, the same one I'd seen them with at The Riverside. Still holding the rifle, the older man went to zip open the bag. He brought back a shiny black laptop.

He sat in my desk chair, rifle dangling from a strap, and opened the laptop.

He plugged the thumb drive into the USB slot and once the icon appeared on the screen, excitedly clicked it to open the drive.

Serge looked like he'd stopped inhaling, he was so nervous. These two men looked desperate. They'd already been chased away from The Riverside when they'd had me in their sites. If they didn't bring back the plane schematic and specs, they could face imprisonment or death when they returned to Russia.

Dmitri ran through the list of files, opening them one by one.

Finally, he scowled and let out an exclamation that I thought must be another curse word.

He turned to me, anger in his eyes.

"Breads and cakes! Rolls! Nothing but recipes." After gesturing angrily, Dmitri threw the thumb drive at me. I flinched when it hit my arm hard and fell to the floor. A red welt rose on my arm.

"It must be here." He leaned toward me, until his face was so close that I could pick up his stale breath, which smelled like onions. "You tell me where, Grace Morrison."

Serge pressed the end of the gun up against my side. I was afraid to move an inch.

I couldn't see a clock, but I estimated that the agents were now forty minutes away. If I could stall Serge and Dmitri, they would still be here when the agents arrived, hopefully armed and ready to take on the two men. I wished there was some way to tell LaValle and Piccelli what they'd be walking into.

"My daughter doesn't know what you're talking about." My father said. "She left Seattle behind. She wanted nothing to do with Ben and the secrets he gave you."

"Shut up, old man." Dmitri pushed my father back against the wall so hard I heard a *thwack* as his head hit. I winced, but my dad sat up and rubbed his head. He seemed to be okay. Biga growled up at Dmitri again.

"After your husband was arrested, we searched your house in Seattle," Dmitri spat out the words, his face red with anger. "We took it apart, piece by piece. And found nothing. There is no other explanation. It must be here."

After looking in the closet, under the bed, and in between the mattresses, then throwing all my books off the shelves, and kicking at the dog toys on the floor, Dmitri seemed ready to move on to another room. Serge herded my father and I down the hall.

I wondered what the point was. Maybe I should just give them the drive. What difference would it really make, aside from Russia getting this lethal bomber? I was exhausted and raw, and wanted this to be over.

These men would take the drive and probably shoot us anyway. But as long as they didn't have the plans, they were dependent on us. If they failed to get their hands on them, they were as good as dead.

The sun was fading, as I saw the darkness creep up outside.

I estimated travel times in my head.

Drive fast, LaValle.

* * *

Dmitri's eyes lit up when he saw my father's office, after he and Serge prodded us down the hall with the black snouts of the assault rifles.

"This! This must be it," he said, when he saw the bulky old desktop computer on the massive oak desk. He eyed the bookshelves and gazed around at the boxes of papers and journals my father had never completely unpacked from our move from Seattle. I could follow Dmitri's thinking. After all, a room jammed with this much stuff must have the drive in it somewhere.

Dmitri pulled out the middle desk drawer and pawed through its contents, throwing items on the floor. He started up the computer. When it would not give him access, he reeled off more Russian swear words.

"Sit," he gestured impatiently with his gun for my dad to take a seat in his chair. My dad, a little shaky on his feet, took a seat, moving his face in range of the computer's camera until the screen unlocked for him and the desktop appeared on the screen.

Hello, John Markley

Dmitri pushed my father out of the way and did a search on the computer, which didn't bring the results he was looking for. He pounded his fist on the desk.

"Look in the drawers," he commanded Serge, while Dmitri stood back, keeping the rifle pointed at my father and me.

Serge pulled out drawers, throwing papers, folders and binders, while Dmitri yelled at him in Russian. The younger man moved on to the filing cabinet and did the same thing.

"I still don't know what you're looking for." I kept my voice as casual as I could.

Dmitri's face was red with frustration. He and Serge weren't going to get this without our help. "A drive? Files? Documents? If I don't know what you two are looking for, I can't help you find it," I said matter-of-factly.

Dmitri's black eyes narrowed into slits. "I believe you are lying, Grace Morrison. I believe you know exactly what we are looking for and where you have hidden it."

He mumbled something in Russian to Serge, who nodded. Both of them stood facing us, guns raised to our chests.

I thought this was the end, but it didn't make sense for them to kill us now. Still, my life of the past eight years did flash through my mind. All the red flags I ignored. My life with Ben had been too good to be true, our travels and our beautiful house financed by money he'd gotten selling defense secrets.

The good things started happening once I decided for myself what I wanted and what I would not put up with.

Serge didn't lower his rifle, but Dmitri did.

"Keep the gun on these two. We're going to the bakery."

Chapter Twenty-Five

Serge pushed my father into the back seat and ordered me into the front passenger seat of the black Lexus, parked behind my car in our carport. Probably because he could easily keep the rifle trained on both of us from his vantage point in the back seat on the driver's side.

When Dmitri started the car, I saw the time. 5:50.

The agents should be ten minutes away. But they'd be headed for our house, not The Laughing Loaf.

For some reason, I'd had an odd hunch it would all come back to the bakery.

Yesterday I remembered what my father had said after he beat me at chess:

Have your moves lined up. Think of what I will do, and be ready to counter it.
I can always predict what you're going to do, dear.

I had my moves lined up. Now we'd see if they worked.

Dmitri used the rental car's GPS, after giving me a

suspicious look when I offered directions. We took the alley, then Dmitri pulled right up by The Laughing Loaf's back step. Serge prodded my father and I out. I pulled out my keys, which I had been carrying around in my pocket all day.

My hand shook a bit as I unlocked the door. I was returning to a place I'd already said a difficult goodbye to.

I walked in, Serge's rifle pointed at my back. How long could I stall? The men were getting desperate and tired. They could get impatient with me and completely lose it and shoot us. I did have bargaining power because they didn't know where the files were—and they assumed I knew exactly where they were. But after coming up with nothing at the house, they'd assumed the files they couldn't find must be here.

"Show us. Now, Grace Morrison." Serge actually poked me in the back with the end of the rifle, and it took all I had not to flinch. Any sudden movement could cause him to shoot. He had too much riding on these files.

I had to stall for time. I was putting a lot of faith in LaValle and Piccelli to figure out where we'd gone.

"Fine." I sighed heavily. "I'll get it. It's in my desk."

I pointed at my tiny office, to make sure they didn't think I was making a run for it. I made my way slowly to the desk, followed closely by the Russians, their guns trained on me and my dad. I took the key out of the compartment in my drawer then reached behind the monitor to push the burner phone compartment key into the lock.

I slowly turned it and flipped it open.

My hands closed around the drive.

I turned around slowly and held it up so the Russians could see a red thumb drive.

Serge pulled his gun away from my side and took in a big breath. He mumbled something in Russian.

Dmitri's face shone like a man given a second chance at life.

"I have seen that drive before, Grace. Now hand it to me."

"Let my father and me go first."

Dmitri and Serge exchanged glances. They could shoot us both now and flee with the drive. But Dmitri would want to check the contents of the drive.

"If you don't believe me, check it with your laptop. My computer's USB drives don't work anymore. I only run my business software on that old thing."

Dmitri paused for a moment. "Let's go out to the car and check it there. Once I verify the files, I will let you go." I wasn't sure he'd let us go, but at least this would buy us time and get us outside.

Serge had his gun to our backs as we followed Dmitri out to the car so he could get the bag with the laptop. I held the thumb drive, under Serge's watchful eye, so he could see I still had it.

Dmitri pulled his laptop out and I handed him the drive, so he could plug it in.

He did and clicked to open the drive. I saw the list of numbered image files displayed on his screen.

"It looks like they're here. Let me try to send." He clicked something on the computer, then waited, then closed his laptop. Sirens whined in the distance. Dmitri's head snapped up and he looked down the alley. "Get in the car, Serge. We'll leave them."

Dmitri got into the driver's seat and Serge slid into the passenger seat. The car revved and lurched forward, accelerating down the alley about fifty feet, only to be blocked by

Piccelli and LaValle, who'd turned into the ally and angled their mountain-style Ford pickup in front of the Lexus.

Right behind them, Chief Westerman pulled up in the River Grove PD squad car. I heard a vehicle coming up behind us, and I turned to see a Santa Cruz County Sheriff's vehicle, coming up the alley from the direction of the Riverside.

Dmitri stumbled out of the Lexus, laptop case and rifle slung over his shoulder.

I took my father's arm. He looked pale and a little wobbly. "Let's watch this from inside. It's going to get wild."

We went inside and watched through the bakery's back door, as Dmitri and Serge fled on foot, back through the line of redwoods, to the river trail. The sheriff and Brad Castro, both visibly armed, followed them. After hesitating, Piccelli, dressed in her ruffled yellow sundress and a jeans jacket, pulled out her gun and headed toward the river herself. I heard gunshots but had no idea who was firing.

Agent LaValle nodded at us through the window and tapped to be let in.

"Gracie and John, I'm glad to see you're safe. We got to your house a little earlier than we expected and immediately got a call from our local contact, who said they saw you take off with the men. The chief pinged us from city hall, saying he saw you in the bakery." LaValle patted my dad on the back. "You had a lot of people keeping an eye on you. Looks like we found you just in time."

I sighed, exhausted, and leaned against the metal table. "The bomber plans are safe. I transferred them to a blue thumb drive, which is now in Biga's treat ball at home. I copied other files onto the red drive yesterday and left it here, just in case I needed it."

LaValle chuckled.

"I just heard from our operatives in DC that the Russians think they have the bomber plans. What did you give them?"

I smiled at them.

"Fifty-seven photographs of Galapagos finches."

* * *

Agent Maura Piccelli met us back at the bakery about an hour later, her "country clothes" muddy and disheveled. But she looked relaxed in a way I hadn't seen before. Maybe the thrill of chasing down bad guys put her in her happy place.

I asked the agents to come up front to the dining area, where I made them lattes and served them reheated scones. I found an ice pack in the freezer for my dad's head and made him a nice hot cup of tea, so he could regain his composure.

It calmed me down to perform these routine tasks—serving people. My heart slowed down to its normal rate, and I began breathing regularly again.

Piccelli sipped her latte and glanced up at LaValle with a smile.

"Dmitri and Serge took off along the river and got about a mile down the trail. They shot a few rounds at us but didn't manage to hit anyone. At one point, they ran into a couple of skunks," she said with a laugh. "Those skunks aimed well. The two men's eyes were stinging and watering. The deputy sheriff was able to arrest them without a fight. His vehicle's going to need some deep cleaning to get that smell out."

I sobered, thinking of Kayden Burnett. "Dmitri told me he killed Kayden Burnett. He bragged about how easy it was. He'd found out that Kayden came here to warn me about them. Kayden's online posts implied that I had something the Russians wanted. Kyle had told him I had it."

"All this after Kayden told everyone you lied about his brother and Ben spying." Piccelli took a sip of her latte and sighed. "Guess he finally accepted the truth."

"Kayden wanted to do something to make up for what happened. And it cost him his life." I thought about Kayden coming to our place in Seattle, a goofy kid, and a bottomless pit when it came to my bread.

LaValle finished the last bite of his scone then picked up the crumbs with his fingers and ate them. "You've done a great job with this place, Gracie."

Finally my father had recovered enough to join the conversation. "Jeremy and Maura, can you tell me what will happen with the two men?" He asked. "They'll be put away for a long time, I would think."

The agents looked at each other, and LaValle answered.

"Since Dmitri and Serge officially came to the US as visitors, they have no diplomatic immunity. They will almost certainly be charged with first degree murder. And with threatening and kidnapping you and Gracie." He frowned and looked down into his latte. "A jury here would likely convict them. They could be returned to Russia at any time in a prisoner swap. That is, if Russia still wants them after this."

My father moved his chair closer to the conversation. His color had returned, and he was holding the ice pack to his head.

"The two men seemed to think if they went back to Russia without the plans, they'd be put in prison," he said. "Or executed."

LaValle nodded. "That's a possibility. We'll be talking

to our sources to see what they've heard. At the least, the men are an embarrassment to their country."

The agents drove us home, where Biga greeted us, shaking with excitement. I carried him in my arms like a furry baby as we walked through the house with the agents, examining the damage done by Dmitri and Serge as they searched for the plans.

"Don't worry, the packers and movers tonight will take care of all this, John and Gracie," Piccelli assured us as we sat in chairs in my father's windowless office. "Though you should pull out and box up anything you'll need for the next week."

My father looked over at me for confirmation. He spoke up this time.

"I believe Gracie and I are thinking the same thing. We don't want to move. We don't want to leave River Grove, and we certainly don't want to move to Alabama."

Tears filled my eyes again, which I hated. I don't cry very often, and I almost never cry in front of people. This time I couldn't stop.

"I don't want to leave River Grove." I choked back a sob. "With the two Russians out of the way, I don't feel in as much danger—"

Piccelli frowned. "Gracie, just because you don't *feel* in danger, doesn't mean you're safe. Yes, those two men have been arrested, but we don't know what will happen in the future."

I breathed in deeply. "The thing is, who *does* know what will happen in the future? Eight years ago, I didn't know I was marrying a man who would sell defense secrets to foreign governments. None of us can predict what will happen to us. But I know that we're part of a community here. I don't want to go somewhere else and start over."

LaValle, still in his beer t-shirt, stared at me, almost in disbelief. "I want to understand this. Are you both saying you want to leave witness protection?"

My father cleared his throat. "No, but I want to stay who we are now, in this town. We have that local contact who's been watching out for us. We have you. Apart from those two idiots in jail, we are doing fine. I'll take my chances."

"Me, too." I nodded.

"But your cover is almost certainly compromised," Piccelli spoke slowly and leaned forward, shaking her head as if our thinking was beyond her. "You do understand that?"

I shrugged. I'd faced death a dozen times already today. "So it means we'll have to be on our guard."

LaValle pulled out his cell phone and made a call, explaining to the moving company that the relocation had been cancelled.

A huge weight lifted off me.

I felt so free and relieved that I wanted to go to The Riverside and dance. I wondered if I would ever be able to do that with Elana again.

For tonight, having this one big thing resolved was enough.

Chapter Twenty-Six

LaValle and Piccelli had been gone for a half an hour when I got a text from Nate. I looked at the time on my phone screen. Sure enough, it was 9 p.m.

As I scrolled through my messages for the first time today, I saw he'd left several messages asking how I was.

Then the one he sent tonight:

A few questions:

1. Are you okay?

2. Will I see you tomorrow at the airport?

3. If you have time, can we talk?

I texted back.

Yes

Yes

YES

When I heard Nate's voice on the phone, my stomach fluttered like a flock of caged pigeons.

I tried hard to keep my voice steady and my feelings on an even keel.

"So you're okay," he said, his voice sounding quiet, tentative. "Your dad's okay. And Biga."

"All of us are fine. A scary thing happened at the bakery today. I'm sure you'll hear about it when you get back, but the bottom line is that the killer of the man on the highway was found, and two men were arrested."

"Okay. So you *were* investigating the death of the man on the highway. And you gave me a hard time last night about risking *my* life to get a good shot."

"Well, I did some looking into the murder," I said weakly, wondering how much power the marshals had to keep my name out of the news. "I mostly talked to Sam Rodriguez about what he saw that morning and then looked up some things online. None of which was that dangerous."

No, it was everything else about my situation that was dangerous. But of course, I didn't say that.

"I'm in Quito tonight, sleeping in a comfortable bed for the first time in a week. I get into SFO at 6:30 tomorrow night. Can't wait to see you, Gracie."

"Thanks for the bird photos. You took some beautiful shots, and I loved looking through them."

I didn't tell him that the officials at the Kremlin had probably seen them, too.

After we hung up, I was wide awake, still rattled by today's events and excited to see Nate tomorrow. I couldn't wait to be back in my bakery tomorrow morning.

I was sure I'd have trouble sleeping, but I conked out quickly.

My dreams that night were about doing normal things

around the bakery. Opening the proofer to see beautiful domes of risen bread and working with Beck in the back room, singing loudly and doing what we both loved.

In peace and without worry.

"C'mon, Biga," I said at 4:25 a.m. the next morning.

I can't remember ever being so happy it was Monday.

"You're coming with me."

I'd bounded out of bed, showering and dressing in record time.

I tossed a treat in his crate. The dog darted in eagerly to get it, then I shut the lid down on the crate quickly.

"Bwahahaha!"

I peered into the grate and gave him my evilest laugh.

I carried him out to the car, where I'd stashed his pen just yesterday, sure I'd be leaving The Laughing Loaf forever.

The cold, sharp air on this clear morning energized me. Stars burned above me, tiny windows of light in the still black sky. There's something I've always loved about baker's hours. Everything at this dark hour belongs to you alone: the open empty roads and the rich smells of a new morning. And the stars and moon above, all stubbornly clinging to their place in the sky.

After all I'd been through in the past seven days, I felt a little like Gandalf in *Lord of the Rings* after he fights the Balrog in Khazad-dûm. Everyone thinks he's dead and gone forever, until he emerges regenerated and triumphant, as Gandalf the White.

As Piccelli had said, we weren't completely safe in River Grove. There could be more threats out there, but I was happy I had survived this one.

When I got into the back room, I set up the dog pen and went back to the car to bring Biga in. I sat on the floor with Biga and played with him in the pen before starting my day, throwing his squeaky toys around and laughing as he raced after them frantically.

I set up an 80s music playlist and cranked up the volume.

There were loaves in the proofer, beautiful brioche loaves I'd bake later this morning, and on the lower racks, my whole wheat biga walnut raisin boules, smelling like fall. After baking bread for seventeen years, I can smell dough and know whether it's on track, and whether it will bake up right. I inhaled the scents of the rich, yeasty dough and sighed in satisfaction.

Then on the counter where Beck set down her basket of eggs in the morning, I saw the envelope I'd left for her yesterday. Her severance check. I pulled the check out and looked at it. I hadn't written anything saying that I was leaving. I didn't say any goodbyes.

It was a large amount. But I could afford it, and Beck was worth investing in. This would be her education fund.

Beck came in at 5:30 a.m. and started singing along to the playlist. She took off her jacket and set down her basket of eggs.

"G'morning, Gracie!" She said brightly.

Then she looked down and saw the envelope.

"What's this?" She turned it over in her hands with a curious smile. "It's for me?"

"Yep." I nodded at her as I rolled out a rectangle of dough for cinnamon rolls.

She opened the envelope and let out a shriek.

"Oh, my God!" She looked at me, her eyes wide. "All of this? What's this for?"

"This is your education fund. This is for you to grow as a baker and pastry chef. Find classes. Go away for a class that looks like something you want to learn to do. If there's something you want to take and it's in San Francisco or New York City, I want you to do it. We'll talk about it and schedule the time. There's also a favor I want to ask you later when the crowds die down."

Beck looked like she was going to either dance for joy or start crying.

"Gracie, you have already done so much for me, just hiring me and letting me invent things."

"Beck, think of it this way." I slathered the cinnamon-butter-brown sugar mixture over the dough. "If people are recommending The Laughing Loaf as a not-to-be-missed place for baked goods, we need to keep our reputation up. You're the Laughing Loaf's secret weapon for coming up with new items. It's a business decision. I'm investing in you."

Beck smiled softly, her lip trembling. "Thank you so much, Gracie."

I clapped my hands together. "We've got a busy morning ahead of us. We're going to have at least twenty-five high schoolers in soon, all amped up for homecoming week. Let's keep the 80s music going and bake."

After Beck showed me her process for making beignets, I had the frying down now, so I took over that task, slipping the dough squares into the hot oil, while keeping an eye on the last rise and bake of the cinnamon rolls. Beck would handle the biggest task at hand—frying up French toast sticks for the high schoolers.

Until almost 7 a.m., we sang and even danced in the back room as we fried, baked, dusted and assembled.

Then I unlocked the front door of the bakery.

It began with a trickle of teens. First, Chloe Westerman and Aiden Franzi, who'd come in to help me with the concert meals last year. They plunked their backpacks down to save their spots at the round table then got in line. Then a flurry of young women came in wearing red and gold RGHS t-shirts. They were followed by a group of teens wearing black jackets and jeans who looked like they vowed to never, ever wear school colors.

Sky and Jeb came in but immediately isolated themselves at separate tables. Sky sat at the round table with the larger group while Jeb went off to a table near the window.

Interesting. The tension between them could hit its peak today.

By 7:30, I counted twenty-nine teens crowded into the bakery dining area, giggling, gossiping, and playing YouTube clips to each other. No one seemed ready to settle down and do schoolwork.

I didn't care. The noise made me happy.

I dispensed French toast sticks and plates of cinnamon rolls, and Beck kept the coffee orders flowing, especially the sweet drinks popular with the high school crowd, like the fruity Cherry Orchard Latte and the chocolate and white chocolate mochas.

Around 8 a.m., I came up to the counter from the back room and heard a loud, angry voice.

"Everything's a fricking joke to you, isn't it? I'm tired of it, Sky."

"What? What did I do?" Sky sat slumped in his chair, looking over at Jeb from heavily lidded eyes. He held a French toast stick between two fingers as if it were a cigar.

"You're making a joke out of the whole homecoming thing." Jeb had his hand in a physics textbook keeping his place as he sat across from a girl who looked like she was hard at work studying, too. "So I got nominated, and you can't just let me do this," Jeb said. "You have to get yourself nominated, too. And walk around town wearing that stupid crown."

"Whaaat?" Sky's voice escalated to a falsetto. "I didn't make people nominate me. So what if they did? They think I'm funny. Everything doesn't have to be all serious."

Jeb shook his head, exasperated. "I can't believe we were ever friends. You've changed, Sky. It's all about getting attention now, isn't it? And you can never get enough."

By this point, every high schooler in the room was listening in to their conversation. Chatter in the room had stopped. This was a show they'd all been binge watching, and judging from what the two young men were saying, there had been many previous episodes.

I left the counter and tapped on Jeb's table, then motioned to Sky.

"Let's have a talk in the back room, guys."

Jeb looked up at me sullenly with an "are you kidding me" face. Sky shrugged and stood up, with a glance around at his audience.

I nodded over at Beck, who'd moved over to the counter to take orders. Jeb and Sky followed me to the back, and I told them to take seats at the metal table.

"What's this all about?" I asked. "Didn't you guys grow up being friends?"

They both nodded. "We live on the same street," Jeb said.

"Our moms are friends. We did everything together growing up. Since we were toddlers." Sky tried to avoid

Jeb's eyes. "Then Jeb ran for student government and started acting like he was better than everybody else."

"Sky started goofing off. Why should I hang out with someone who doesn't care about school? And makes fun of me?"

"You do know that when you grow up, people change, right?" I paused to pull a tray of scones out of the oven and started transferring them to the cooling racks. "That's how it works. Life after high school is different. People get new interests. They get new friends. Chloe said you guys are going away to college next year. Where?"

Jeb's face brightened. "I'm going back east. Boston."

"Just down the road. Cal State Monterey Bay," Sky said with a smirk.

"Totally different places. High school throws everybody together in a small fishbowl whether you like it or not, especially in River Grove. But after you've been away for a while, who knows. Maybe you'll be friends again, like when you were kids. Something that bugs you now won't seem as important. Or you'll have some distance to laugh about it."

"Yeah, I don't know about that." Jeb shot a dark look at Sky.

"I'm not doing the homecoming thing just to bug you, Jeb. I got nominated and thought it was hilarious. I went with it. I'm not Mr. Popular like you are."

I turned to face them. "Okay, guys. I've got things to bake. I need you to go out there and be civil with each other. Can you do it?"

Jeb shrugged and looked down at his shoes.

Sky mumbled. "I *guess.*"

The two went back out to the dining area and took their seats, and I relieved Beck at the counter. I didn't hear any further argument from the two. When the high schoolers poured out onto the street at 8:15 a.m., Sky and Jeb were walking and laughing with a group of three other students.

As River Grove's adult population made their way in, I passed by Beck and whispered. "I wanted them to stop fighting, but it's been so long, I'm not sure I'm qualified to give advice to high schoolers."

She laughed as she prepared the espresso machine for another drink. "Gracie, I was homeschooled with my brothers. You're way more qualified than I am."

It's funny what a reprieve will do for you. I went through the day feeling grateful. I savored my conversations with the bakery regulars. The smells of everything baking made me happier than usual. Routine chores didn't seem as tedious. When the chief came in with Mayor C, he flashed me a big smile. I wonder if the fed's local contact, whoever that was, had given him a heads-up last night that we weren't leaving.

When the crowd thinned at 10:30, and customers in the bakery had been served, I pulled Beck into the back room.

"I wanted to ask you a favor, Beck. And it's kind of a big one."

"What is it?" She looked a little worried.

"I know this will require some preparation from both of us." I watched her brow furrow. "I want to leave you in charge of the bakery for two days."

Beck looked unable to speak. Her lips quivered. "But—how would I do that? I can open and close. But I haven't done scones or cinnamon rolls yet. And all the bread cycles—"

"We'll work on that. Maybe we'll streamline things for those days and focus less on the bread. I'll look for some extra help in the morning for the bakery, too. We're doing more business, and it's about time."

Beck's lips turned up in a tentative smile. "You think I can do this."

I laughed. "Of course you can."

"It wouldn't be, like, tomorrow or anything."

"No, it wouldn't, Beck."

It would take some planning to pull off. But I needed a life outside the bakery. And Beck was ready to learn and take on more in her assistant manager role.

Now that we were staying in River Grove, and The Laughing Loaf was going to continue, it made sense to plan for growing the business.

Especially if we continued to draw in those out-of-town customers.

Assuming Mayor C and the chief's traffic plans allowed for it.

Chapter Twenty-Seven

A
t 4:30 p.m., I left River Grove on my way to San Francisco International Airport.

My father had invited Mary Jo Hartman over to cook an elaborate steak dinner *with* him, which sounded like something I wanted to watch later on video.

I was in no hurry to get home.

As I drove north on Highway 1, the ocean was still visible, its undulating waters dappled by gold and orange as the sun slipped lower down the horizon. After the intensity of the past week, the view and the solitude of the car felt comforting.

Even though we were safe for now, and I'd savored every minute of my day at the bakery, I felt a pang of sadness for Kayden Burnett. His death was a loss, another casualty of my ex-husband and his friend's scheme for selling defense secrets.

My father and I had been fortunate—the two Russians hadn't killed us, mostly because we had something they wanted very badly. If I hadn't figured out how to make them think they were getting the bomber plans, we'd be dead, too.

I felt the loss of my friend. I wanted to share more with Elana and continue being her friend. I wished I could tell her the real story of what had happened this week, as opposed to what she'd read in the River Grove Gazette or hear from people in town.

As the twisting Highway 92 poured me onto 101 North, I got that giddy feeling again as I thought about seeing Nate. If this week of being away from him had been a test, I'd failed it. I'd thought about him a lot. And really-- I'd done a lame job of ghosting him.

I approached Arrivals at SFO and pulled as close to the crowded pickup lane as I could get, then waited, praying I wouldn't get prodded by security to move on. In about five minutes, a very tanned Nathaniel Behrens walked out of the automatic doors with a backpack and camera bag over his shoulder as he scanned the line of waiting cars.

When I honked, he grinned and jogged over to my car. After he stowed his pack and camera bag in the back seat and slid into the passenger seat, I moved toward him over the gear shift and planted a nice long kiss on *his* lips. He smelled fresh, like limes and the ocean.

"Red alert. Security guys are actually watching us now," Nate glanced over at the curb after we broke away.

"Guess I missed that 'no kissing' sign on the curb." I prepared myself to merge into the flow of traffic. "So let's go. Where to?"

"Let's find a place on the coast for dinner. Does that sound good to you?"

Tonight, I felt open. And ready to take Reggie's advice to enjoy this moment as long as it lasted. We drove back on Highway 92, and I eased us in and out of the curves through the coastal mountains as we talked about Nate's adventures in the Galapagos and, in modified form, what had happened at The Laughing Loaf yesterday.

After Nate found a seafood restaurant in Half Moon Bay, we pulled into the lot and parked, looking out at the ocean. The sun had just faded into the horizon, and I could see the foamy waves in the growing darkness looking like Cheshire Cat teeth as they lapped the sand.

Before we went inside, Nate sat for a moment looking over at me, his face lit by the neon light of the restaurant's sign.

"I wasn't sure I'd see you again. After that phone call when you said *if something happens to me.*"

I smiled at him and shook my head.

"I panicked. I wanted you to know how I felt about you. Just in case."

He reached over and laid his warm hand over mine. I saw something in his eyes that I hadn't seen before. It reminded me of the impasse I'd had when talking to the chief, when both of us knew more than we were allowed to say.

"Hey, I'm getting Beck ready to fill in for me for a few days. I'm really looking forward to that getaway."
Nate smiled, and it reminded me of the waves glowing in the dark.
"Me, too, Grace."

THE END

Thank you!

Are you in a book club?

Are you in a book club?
Interested in reading any of The Laughing Loaf Bakery
Mysteries? I'd love to appear at your book club online - or in
person, if you're in the San Francisco Bay Area.
Contact me at thelaughingloaf@gmail.com

Also by Victoria Kazarian

Drop Dead Bread - Laughing Loaf Bakery Mystery #1

Bread to Rights - Laughing Loaf Bakery Mystery #2

Look for *Sourdough and Cyanide* - Laughing Loaf Bakery Mystery #4, coming Fall 2023.

Traditional mystery

(Detectives Jimmy Ruiz and Dani Grasso):

Swift Horses Racing – Silicon Valley Murder Book 1

Across the Red Sky – Silicon Valley Murder Book 2

A Tree of Poison – Silicon Valley Murder Book 3

About Victoria Kazarian

Victoria Kazarian lives and writes in San Jose, California. After working for years as a Silicon Valley marketing professional, she taught high school English and actually owned a bread bakery of her own called The Laughing Loaf. When she's not writing, she enjoys baking artisan breads and forcing her children and dog to go on road trips to the Pacific Northwest.

See what she's up to at victoriakazarian.com

You can contact Victoria—or perhaps leave a message for Gracie Markley herself—at TheLaughingLoaf@gmail.com

Acknowledgments

Thank you to my copy editor and idea tester, Honest Magpie, aka Armen Kazarian, for their hard work on this book, honest critiques. and attention to details. And for bringing us Peewee, the cutest Chihuahua-Basenji mix around and the model for Gracie's Biga.

Thank you to the beta readers who made this book better: Faye Friesen Myers, Pam Milliken, and Chris Anderson.

Thank you to Mary Ann Askins, whose ability to find typos and inconsistencies—while giving words of cheery encouragement—helped me tremendously with this book.

Thank you to Debbie Cunningham for being my awesome book evangelist on her travels around the world.

To the organization Sisters in Crime—SinC National, the Guppies group and the Coastal Cruisers and NorCal chapters—thank you. Ditto to the phenomenal 20Books-to50K organization. I would not be published if it weren't for you all.

Thanks to my husband, Pete, for his encouragement and for being really good at picking up take-out food.

And to my siblings, Pam, Kerry and Matt, for their support and for inspiring me with their own creative gifts.

* * *

Whole Wheat Walnut Raisin Biga Bread

Total time: 16-18 hours
Makes one loaf

With a biga, you're allowing the first part of the bread mixture to ferment and develop flavors before you add the rest of the ingredients. It's a way to get richer flavor without a sourdough starter. Also, it's not sour!

The biga for this loaf is made of white flour, while the remainder is mostly whole wheat flour. It's a hearty and savory bread.

This recipe doesn't take much work, but it does take time. The biga ferments for 11-12 hours, which is usually overnight. You'll then have a couple of other short rises after that.

NOTE: When you're baking bread, an oven temperature gauge is a great thing to have. Then you'll know what temperatures your oven is really baking at and make adjustments (home ovens can vary). I have an inexpensive one from Target, and it works just fine.

Biga (overnight pre-ferment)

Whole Wheat Walnut Raisin Biga Bread

Mix the following in a 4-8 quart plastic or ceramic container:

1-1/2 cups white flour (can be all-purpose flour, but bread flour will give you more rise)
3/4 cup warm water
1/8 teaspoon dried yeast

Mix together. It will be a little shaggy looking. Cover the top with stretch wrap and then a kitchen towel. Set in a warm place (72 degrees) for 11-12 hours.

After this, take off the covering. The *biga* will have risen and smoothed out. It will have a faint alcohol scent.

Now add:

1 cup + 1 tablespoon whole wheat flour
1 half cup white flour
1 cup + 1 tablespoon of warm water
1-1/2 teaspoons of sea salt
3/4 teaspoon dried yeast
2 tablespoons molasses

Mix these until blended. The dough will be sticky!
Use your pointer finger and thumb as pincers to cut/separate the dough into ping-pong-sized balls. Then squish the balls together. Do this about 3-4 times until you can see the mixture becoming a more homogenous color.
Then you'll add:

¾ cup of chopped walnuts
¾ cup of raisins

Fold these into the dough until well distributed.

Cover the mixture in the container with plastic stretch wrap then a kitchen towel. Put back into your warm place for 3 hours—this is the bulk rise. Dough is ready when it's almost tripled in size.

After the bulk rise:

Dump dough out onto a very lightly floured surface and round it out with your hands. There should be some friction between the dough and the surface. Shape the dough, cupping the bread with your hands to push the bottom sides of the dough in, while turning the ball in a circular motion on the surface. This should result in a tighter, more compact ball of dough. When you have a nicely rounded ball, place a kitchen towel in a medium-sized mixing bowl and flour it. Then place the ball in the bowl and let rise in a warm place for one hour.

Meanwhile, place a cast-iron pot (one that has a lid) or dutch oven in the oven on the middle rack, sprinkle corn meal lightly over the inside bottom of the pot, and preheat the oven to 475 degrees.

After the oven's come to temperature, open the oven and wearing an oven mitt, carefully set your dough ball into the heated pot. Immediately cover the pot with its lid. Bake for 28 minutes.

After 28 minutes, take off the lid and allow the loaf to cook uncovered for about 5 minutes till nicely browned.

Then carefully, wearing oven mitts, take the pot out of the oven. Remove the loaf from the pot and place on a cooling rack. Don't slice for an hour. Then enjoy. Tastes great with good butter and even better slathered with cream cheese.

Whole Wheat Walnut Raisin Biga Bread

* * *

Cherry Orchard Latte

Cherry Orchard Latte

A sweet drink that high schoolers and Police Chief Westerman love. The addition of the peach syrup and the whipped cream-orange zest on top helps balance the flavors.

In coffee mug/cup, mix two shots of espresso or strong coffee (a jigger or about ¼ cup per shot) with:

¼ cup milk or half-and-half of your choice
2 tablespoons cherry Torani syrup
1 tablespoon peach Torani syrup

Top with whipped cream and orange zest

Beck's Caramel Apple Tarts

Tastes like fall. Homey and delicious.

Total time: 1 hour, 20 minutes
Makes 6 small 4-inch tarts (or one regular-sized tart)
Preheat over to 350 degrees.

Filling:

4 Granny Smith apples, peeled, cored and sliced
Put in 2 quart bowl, then add:
Juice of 1 lemon – As soon as the apples are sliced, coat them with this so they don't brown.

Then add the following ingredients and mix so the apples are evenly coated with them.
  Then cover bowl with plastic wrap and let them marinate while you make the crust.

1/3 cup brown sugar
1 tsp cinnamon

½ tsp ground ginger
¼ tsp cloves
¼ tsp nutmeg
¼ tsp kosher or sea salt
1 tsp vanilla extract

Crust:

1-1/3 cup all-purpose flour (also works well with cup-for-cup mix of gluten-free flour)
¼ packed brown sugar
½ teaspoon kosher or sea salt
¼ cinnamon
9 tbsp butter, melted

Mix the dry ingredients well, then pour in the melted butter. Mix together until it forms a dough. Use your fingers to press mixture into six lightly greased 4" tart pans or a full-sized 10" tart pan. If you don't have tart pans, use cupcake tins. It'll be harder to fit the filling in, but you can do it--and they'll taste just as good.

Place the marinated apples into the crusts. For the 4" tarts, you can lay them in a fan pattern on the crust or break the apple slices in half and arrange them in a spiral. If you're making a full-sized tart, overlap the full apple slices in concentric circles in the pan.

Baking:

If you're making the small tart pans, lay the filled tart pans on a baking sheet.

Cut two tablespoons of butter into small pieces and dot the top of the tart(s) with it. Then sprinkle a tablespoon full of sugar over the tart(s).

For the small tarts, bake for 40 minutes. For the large tart, bake for an hour.

Halfway through the bake, if the crust is getting too dark, lay a sheet of aluminum foil over the baking sheet or tart pan.

Topping:

Right after you remove the tart(s) from the oven, heat ¼ cup of caramel sauce or caramel ice cream topping about 15 seconds in microwave. Brush this over the baked tart(s).

Enjoy the tarts by themselves or with a scoop of ice cream!

Shepherd's Pie

Gracie's father loves this comfort food dish, especially in the cool fall weather. Shepherd's Pie is supposed to be made with ground lamb, not beef—when you make it with ground beef, it's called Cottage Pie.

Not a battle worth fighting since most people call the ground beef Shepherd's Pie anyway. And both versions taste great!

There are two parts to this dish: the mashed potato topping and the meat/vegetable filling.

Topping:

You'll need to make four cups of mashed potatoes. You can use instant mashed potatoes— no shame in that! Make sure you're generous with adding butter to them and a 1/4 cup of sour cream, though, to enrich the flavor.

Whether you're making the potatoes from scratch or a box, have on hand about 1/2 cup of grated cheese, a few slices of bacon, chopped, and a tablespoon or two of chopped chives—to sprinkle across the top after you take it out of the oven.

Mashed potatoes:
3 large russet potatoes, peeled and diced
1/3 cup of whole milk or half and half
6-8 tablespoons butter
1/2 teaspoon garlic powder
1/2 teaspoon salt

Making sure they're well covered by water, cook the diced potatoes in a large pot until they fall apart when you stick a fork in them. Then drain them in a large colander to get rid of excess water. Put them back in the pot and add butter, folding it in till it's melted. Add the half and half, then use a potato masher or mix at low speed with a hand mixer till they're smooth.

Set aside until you're ready to cover the filling.

Filling:

4 slices of bacon
Two large carrots, chopped
Two ribs of celery, chopped
1 onion, diced
1/2 cup chopped portobello or crimini mushrooms
2 pounds of ground lamb OR ground beef
1 teaspoon sea or kosher salt
1/2 teaspoon black pepper
2 teaspoons thyme leaves
1 teaspoon oregano
1 teaspoon chopped rosemary
1 tablespoon Worcestershire sauce

3 tablespoons tomato paste

1-3/4 cups chicken or beef broth

1 tablespoon corn starch

Preheat oven to 375 degrees.

In a large pot on medium heat, cook bacon slices, then drain all but a tablespoon of the grease and add carrots, celery and onion. Stir and cook in the grease over medium heat until the onions are transparent and the carrots and celery are slightly soft, then add the mushrooms and cook till softened. Now add the ground meat and cook till done, draining off the grease. Add salt, pepper, thyme, oregano and rosemary—and the broth, Worcestershire sauce, and tomato paste. Stir till everything's blended, then sprinkle corn starch over the mixture and continue cooking and stirring till it thickens. Pour the mixture into a medium casserole dish.

Now dollop the surface of the filling in the casserole dish with generous blobs of mashed potatoes. Once you've put all the blobs on, smooth them out so the surface of the casserole is covered by about an inch of mashed potatoes. Sprinkle with cheese and bacon if you wish. Bake for 30-35 minutes, until the mashed potato topping browns. Then take out of the oven and top with chives.

This is a great recipe to make ahead, stash in your fridge, then bake up the next night. If you do this, bake a little longer—35-40 minutes.

* * *

Follow me!

Follow me on Facebook at **Victoria Kazarian - author** for additional recipes I'll be posting from *The Laughing Loaf Bakery Mysteries.*

* * *

www.ingramcontent.com/pod-product-compliance
Lightning Source LLC
Chambersburg PA
CBHW070509300726
48975CB00007B/2378